He pulled Kim to her feet and then into his arms.

They landed body to body and, mercy, every part of him was well aware of that. This hug might be for comfort, but it was impossible for him not to feel other things. Judging from the slight silky hitch of her breath, she was feeling them as well.

"I would say this was a bad idea if it didn't feel so good," she murmured.

He was in complete agreement with her. Theo didn't push things though. He definitely didn't put his mouth against her cheek even though that was what he wanted to do. However, he did draw in her scent, which, of course, gave him another hit of heat.

They stayed there, pressed against each other, with his breathing picking up the rhythm of hers. That helped, too. Because it felt like they were together on even that most basic level. Along with the heat, he could feel his nerves leveling off. Could feel some of the tightness ease up in his muscles.

It didn't last.

LAST SEEN IN SILVER CREEK

USA TODAY Bestselling Author
DELORES FOSSEN

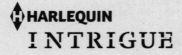

HARLEQUIN
INTRIGUE

HARLEQUIN®

INTRIGUE™

Recycling programs for this product may not exist in your area.

ISBN-13: 978-1-335-59108-1

Last Seen in Silver Creek

For questions and comments about the quality of this book, please contact us at CustomerService@Harlequin.com.

Harlequin Enterprises ULC
22 Adelaide St. West, 41st Floor
Toronto, Ontario M5H 4E3, Canada
www.Harlequin.com

Printed in U.S.A.

Delores Fossen, a *USA TODAY* bestselling author, has written over one hundred novels, with millions of copies of her books in print worldwide. She's received a Booksellers' Best Award and an RT Reviewers' Choice Best Book Award. She was also a finalist for a prestigious RITA® Award. You can contact the author through her website at www.deloresfossen.com.

Books by Delores Fossen

Harlequin Intrigue

Silver Creek Lawmen: Second Generation

Targeted in Silver Creek
Maverick Detective Dad
Last Seen in Silver Creek

The Law in Lubbock County

Sheriff in the Saddle
Maverick Justice
Lawman to the Core
Spurred to Justice

Mercy Ridge Lawmen

Her Child to Protect
Safeguarding the Surrogate
Targeting the Deputy
Pursued by the Sheriff

Visit the Author Profile page at Harlequin.com.

CAST OF CHARACTERS

Sheriff Theo Sheldon—As the new sheriff of Silver Creek, he must face down the killer who murdered his parents while protecting the killer's new target.

Kim Ryland—An assistant district attorney who clearly has a killer after her. She must team up with Theo, the very man she's spent a lifetime avoiding because of their painful shared past.

Jack Sheldon—Theo's two-year-old son with his ex-wife. Theo will do whatever it takes to make sure he's safe.

Faith Sheldon—Theo's kid sister who was kidnapped twenty-one years ago when she was twelve. Last seen in Silver Creek, has Faith finally returned, or is the woman claiming to be Faith an imposter?

Greg Conner—He's engaged to the woman he believes is Theo's missing sister, but he's keeping secrets.

Duran Davidson—Greg's lawyer. There are rumors he's involved in black market adoptions and could have arranged to have Faith kidnapped all those years ago.

Quill Odell—He's out of prison on bail awaiting trial for domestic assault, and Kim is the prosecuting attorney for the case. He could be behind the attempts on Kim's life.

Chapter One

Kim Ryland fought to get out of the nightmare. It came at her in pieces that were as brittle and sharp as razors.

"Hide," he told her. "Hide now."

And that's what she'd done. What she was doing in one of those brittle dream pieces that stabbed and sliced its way through her. In the dream, she clutched the stuffed dog against her and dropped down onto the floor, scuttling under the bed and clamping her teeth over her bottom lip so the killer couldn't hear any of the sounds she might make.

Like that night when the nightmare had been real, Kim didn't hear much going on in the house. Couldn't. Not with her heartbeat crashing in her ears. But she could feel. Mercy, could she. Both then and now. And what she felt was something no eight-year-old child should ever have to experience.

Terror.

On a hard gasp, Kim finally woke, struggling to get to a sitting position while she fought for breath. Fought to get her throat unclamped. She was in her bedroom. Alone and safe. She was no longer a child.

And no killer was coming for her tonight.

Kim glanced at the clock and groaned. It was barely four in the morning. Considering the late night she'd put in preparing a case she'd be prosecuting, she needed at least a couple more hours of sleep. Sleep she clearly wouldn't get, not with her body still revving from the nightmare.

Apparently, nightmares didn't have an expiration date since she'd been having this particular one for twenty-one years now. Since she'd been eight and had cowered under her best friend's pink bed during a sleepover.

Those images of what had happened back then had now gotten mixed up with her current case. Well, one of them anyway. As the assistant district attorney in her hometown of Silver Creek, Texas, she always had several cases on her proverbial plate, rarely one as serious, though, as the domestic aggravated assault trial that was coming up in four days. There'd been plenty of violence in that crime, too, which was probably why the dream had come at her so hard tonight.

Cursing her memories and the dull headache that was now throbbing nonstop, Kim threw back the covers, dragged on the silky blue robe her mom had given her for Christmas, grabbed her phone to check her emails, and made her way to the kitchen. Just walking through her house soothed her.

Some.

This was home, filled with the things that reminded her that she'd come from a loving, protective family. Heirloom furniture. Framed pictures of those family members on the mantel. The patchwork quilt throw that her great-grandmother had made. All pieces that canceled out that nightmare. Well, mostly they did. The nightmare and memories were always there, lurking just beneath the surface.

Kim programmed some strong coffee, planning to drink the entire pot herself. She wasn't sure she could focus yet on her laptop screen so, after she glanced at her emails and didn't see anything pressing, she picked up the stack of mail from the kitchen counter. Obviously, one of her parents had picked it up at the post office for her, a reminder that it had been a while since she'd checked the box herself. Not her folks though. They checked often and brought over hers since they had keys to both the post office box and her house.

With the coffee maker sputtering and pumping out the much-needed caffeine, she dragged the trash can from under the sink and started going through the mail, automatically tossing the sales papers and the junk. Then she froze and stared at the letter that'd been in the middle of the pile.

And she knew exactly what it was.

Oh, God.

Kim didn't open it, didn't touch it. Instead, she pulled out her phone and, without hesitating, called Sheriff Theo Sheldon. Despite the early hour, he answered on the second ring.

"Kim?" he said, sounding plenty groggy. Not so groggy, though, since he hadn't missed seeing her name on his phone screen. "What's wrong?"

"I got another letter," she managed to say, though her hands and voice were now trembling a little.

"I'm on my way," Theo assured her, and in that instant, the grogginess had vanished.

Kim murmured a thanks and the moment she ended the call, she used her phone to snap a picture of the envelope. Something she'd done for the other eight letters she'd received over the years. She copied the image to the online storage file where she had photos of the others, and she pulled those up now to verify that this one was indeed the same. Not that she needed verification, but it gave her something to do while she waited for Theo.

Yes, this one was the same.

A plain white envelope. No return address. Kim's name and post office address had been typed on an old-fashioned typewriter. Or rather "Kimmie" had been typed.

Her childhood nickname.

Also like the other letters, the stamp was affixed sideways in the upper right-hand corner. Maybe the position was some kind of message or clue, but if that was the case, Kim and the Silver Creek Sheriff's Office hadn't been able to figure out what it meant. It was possible the sender had positioned it that way just to play mind games with her since the figures on the stamps weren't upright but rather on their sides.

Like a dead person might be.

All the other letters had been analyzed, of course, and the lab had identified plenty of smudged prints and even some trace DNA, but not enough to attempt to find a match in any of the databases. Maybe this one would be different, though she had to imagine it'd been handled by plenty of people just to have made it into her post office box.

She considered calling her uncle Grayson, who up until the past two months had been the sheriff of Silver Creek for more than three decades. This was his case, too. Always would be. But a call could wait until a more decent hour. Ditto for the one she'd need to make to her folks.

Kim knew full well that she wouldn't be able to delay either of those particular calls much more than an hour or two since it wouldn't take long for word to get out that she'd gotten another letter. And she'd need to do some soothing there. Some reassuring. Of course, any reassurance she could give her parents and her uncle would be a lie, but she didn't want any of them to know that these letters and the memories they stirred up were still eating away at her.

But they were.

They always would.

Still, her parents didn't need to add any more layers to the guilt they no doubt felt at not being able to prevent their little girl from being caught up in the events of that tragic night. A night where two people had been murdered and Kim's best friend, Faith, had disappeared. The killer had taken her, and Kim was well aware that it could have been her instead of Faith.

Kim got herself that much-needed mug of coffee and went back to her bedroom to pull on a pair of jeans, a flannel shirt and shoes. It was best for her to be fully dressed when dealing with Theo. Mentally dressed, too. There was always that stir of heat between them. A forbidden fruit kind of thing, and it just wasn't a good idea for her to test that forbiddance or the heat tonight. Not when she was already feeling a little dinged and jittery.

With her clothing "armor" in place, Kim walked to the front window to keep watch for Theo. It was still dark, but there was a fingernail moon so she could see the cold January wind battering the now bare trees around her property. And just like that, she got another whiplash of memories.

It'd been cold that other night, too, and when her father had carried her out of the house, Kim had heard the frost crunch beneath his boots. He'd cradled her against him just as Grayson had done the same to Theo. Except Grayson hadn't actually picked up Theo, who'd been twelve at the time. Instead, Grayson had put a protective arm around him, leading Theo to the waiting cruiser. That protection had continued when Grayson and his wife, Eve, had taken Theo to live with them rather than put him into the foster care system.

The people who hadn't gotten led out of the Sheldon house by the Ryland family that night were Theo's parents and his sister, Faith. No escape for them. Kim hadn't actually seen Faith being kidnapped or the bodies of Theo's parents. Only the blood smeared on the floor.

So much blood.

She'd only glimpsed it, peeking out even after her father had told her to keep her eyes shut as he'd carried her from the house. Kim wished she'd obeyed. Wished the image of all those blood smears wasn't in her head.

Yes, she was definitely feeling dinged and jittery.

Because Kim had read all the reports of the murders and the kidnapping, she knew plenty had been done to try to find the killer and what happened to Faith. There'd been an extensive search, and Faith's photo had been added in every available missing persons database. With no results. Faith had simply disappeared.

The sudden slash of headlights caused her attention to snap to the road where she saw Theo's truck pull into her driveway. She'd figured it wouldn't take him long to get there since he lived only a half mile away and was her closest neighbor. Then again, if his two-year-old son Jack, had been staying the night, Theo would have needed to let the boy's nanny know he was heading out. That could have tacked on a minute or two to his travel time.

She watched Theo park and step out of his truck, his gaze automatically going to the window to meet hers. If he was feeling any dings or signs of needing hits of caffeine, he wasn't showing them.

Just the opposite.

Even though he likely would have dressed in a hurry, nothing about him was askew. He was wearing his usual jeans, a gray work shirt and a black Stetson that she knew had once belonged to his father. It was well worn and fit as if it'd been custom made for him.

The moonlight flickered on the badge he had clipped to his belt. A shiny silver star that was only two months old and had come with his new job title of sheriff of Silver Creek. It occurred to her that even without the badge, he looked like the cowboy cop that he was. Always had. Some people were born old. Theo had been born to be a Silver Creek lawman.

He flipped up the collar of his buckskin coat and made his way across the yard and to her porch. The relentless wind whipped against the ends of his dark blond hair, and he had to press his hand to his Stetson to stop it from flying. Kim set her coffee aside so she could disengage the security system and unlock the door for him.

"Thanks for coming so fast," she greeted. "I wasn't sure if you had Jack tonight or not."

"No. He's with Nadia."

Nadia, Theo's ex and Jack's mom. Nadia also had other "labels," such as Kim's former best friend. Emphasis on the *former*. But that wasn't something Kim intended to give any more thought to right now.

Theo stepped in, bringing with him the cold and fresh scent of the frost. It blended with the leather from his coat and his body heat. Yes, even now there was heat.

"The letter's on the counter," Kim said, shutting the door. "I'll get you some coffee."

He muttered a thanks and made a beeline to the counter. The sigh he made when he saw the envelope was long and laced with weariness.

"I'm not sure when the letter arrived," Kim went on. She handed him his coffee. "According to the postmark, it was mailed from Dallas five days ago." A six-hour drive from Silver Creek. That didn't mean that's where the sender lived though. In fact, Kim was betting the person had no connection to Dallas that could be traced back to whoever had sent it.

Theo made a sound to acknowledge that he'd heard her, and he sipped his coffee while he studied the envelope. "You're either staying up late or getting up early," he remarked.

"Getting up early. Dreams," she tacked onto that.

He turned his intense blue eyes toward her and she saw that he knew what she meant. Not *dreams* but rather the nightmare.

"Yeah," he said. Theo repeated that *yeah* under his breath. "Sometimes, I save them in the dreams. *Sometimes*," he added in a murmur that let her know that didn't happen nearly often enough.

It wouldn't do any good for her to remind him that he'd been just twelve years old. A kid. And that if he'd tried to rescue his parents from that unidentified intruder/killer, he would likely also have been murdered.

That's what had come darn close to happening, too.

When the cops and CSIs had pieced together the crime scene, they'd surmised that the killer had managed to get out of the house mere seconds before Theo had come running down the stairs with a baseball bat. Since the killer had obviously had a weapon, one that he'd used on Theo's parents, he likely wouldn't have hesitated to use it on Theo as well.

"You saved me," Kim reminded him instead. His *hide now* order had worked. Kim had hidden, and the killer hadn't found her.

The next sound Theo made definitely wasn't one of agreement. This conversation was picking at the old wounds, bringing everything back to the surface, and in Theo's mind, the *surface* didn't paint him in a good light. He'd been too late to save his parents or to stop the killer from kidnapping his sister when she'd apparently been coming out of the hall bathroom. Too late to try to stop the killer-kidnapper from fleeing the scene.

Because Kim had obeyed Theo's shouted order of *hide now*, Kim hadn't seen the killer, and because of the thudding in her ears, she hadn't heard the chaos of that night. Hadn't heard Faith scream for help. But apparently Theo had. Kim had read the reports, and he'd heard his kid sister calling out for him.

Help me, Theo. Help me.

A therapist would probably pretty it up a little, but Kim knew something like that could mess you up for the rest of your life. It'd certainly done a number on Theo, and he was carrying a lot of guilt because of it.

Theo drank a long gulp of coffee, put aside the cup and took out a pair of gloves and an evidence bag from his coat pocket. "Dallas," he said, obviously looking at the postmark again. "The first two came from there."

Yes, and the others had been postmarked from other Texas cities. Emphasis on *cities*. Not from small towns like Silver Creek where someone might have noticed a stranger or someone suspicious mailing a letter.

Like the other envelopes, this one hadn't actually been sealed the traditional way. The flap had instead been taped down, ensuring that no one had licked it and therefore no one had left behind any DNA from saliva.

There'd been no DNA, prints or fibers previously left on the tape either.

Theo carefully slid out the single folded sheet of white paper that was the textbook definition of plain and nondescript. The message, however, was anything but. Even though Kim steeled herself up, it felt like the gut punch that it was.

"'Help me. Please help me,'" Theo read aloud.

A variation of the words that Faith had shouted the night she'd been taken twenty-one years ago when both Faith and Kim had been eight. Like the other letters Kim had received, this particular plea had been typed, and there was no signature. No explanation as to why the letter had been sent to Kim and not Theo.

Kim gave a resigned sigh, knowing that even though the letters hadn't been sent to him, the gut punch was there for Theo, too. But Theo wasn't sighing. He unfolded the bottom third of the letter and leaned in to examine the right corner. Kim leaned in, as well, until her head was against Theo's, and she saw what he was looking at.

The tiny rust-colored dot.

It was about half the size of a grain of rice. So small that Kim might have missed it had it not caught Theo's attention.

"That could be blood," he murmured.

That got her heart revving because it certainly looked like dried blood to her. There'd been nothing like that on the others, but maybe this meant Faith—or whoever was doing this—had left a little piece of herself or himself behind.

"I'll get it to the lab ASAP," Theo said, refolding the letter and putting it in the evidence bag. He took out a pen, no doubt to label the bag, but a sound stopped him cold.

Somewhere, outside the house, a woman screamed.

Chapter Two

The moment Theo heard the scream, his cop instincts kicked in. He whipped his gun from his holster and automatically caught onto Kim's arm to move her behind him before they raced to the front window. Theo kept her behind him, too, when he peered out into the darkness.

Nothing.

He certainly didn't see a woman. But judging from the sound of that scream, she was nearby.

"Stay inside," Theo warned Kim as he opened the door so he could step onto the porch.

"I think the sound came from the east side of the house," Kim provided, and he heard the worry in her voice.

Theo was worried, too. Kim's property wasn't exactly on the beaten path, and it was a good mile away from town. On a cold night like this, a person would have needed a vehicle to get there. Only a person who was in a whole lot of trouble let out a scream like that.

Of course, there was another possibility. It was the tail end of Christmas break, and it was possible some bored teenagers wanted to play a prank on the town's assistant DA who lived alone out here. He was really hoping that was all there was to it. But it felt like more. It felt like something bad.

With his gun still drawn, Theo stepped back out into that bitter cold and went down the porch steps so he could have a look around the sprawling yard. There were plenty of trees, shrubs and large brick-lined flower beds that were now empty, but nothing looked out of place.

"I'm Sheriff Theo Sheldon," he yelled. "Who's out there?"

He waited, listening for anything, including the sound of running footsteps from pranking teenagers, but he heard nothing that didn't belong to the night. The wind, the creak and slap of the tree branches, the deep stuttering rhythm of a hooting owl. Some owls could sound like a human screeching. Other animals could, too. But Theo mentally replayed that scream he'd heard.

No. It hadn't come from an animal.

Theo glanced back to make sure Kim was staying put. She was, sort of. She'd come out onto the porch, and with her arms wrapped around herself and no doubt shivering from the cold, she was firing glances all around, especially on the east side of the house. There were plenty of trees and shrubs there, too, and a barn surrounded by a corral.

"Did you leave the barn doors open?" Theo asked her.

"Yes. I wanted my horses to be able to go in if it got too cold for them."

Since the barn was on the east side of the property

and therefore in the direction where they'd heard the scream, that's where Theo headed. Right toward those open doors.

"Wait," Kim insisted. "Let me grab a coat and I'll go with you."

He didn't especially want her to do that, but Theo wasn't a fan of leaving her alone either. The downside to being a cop and the survivor of a home invasion was that he could imagine all sorts of worst-case scenarios.

Hell, he'd lived through worst cases.

And while having Kim with him also wasn't an ideal solution, neither was leaving her alone. After all, one of those worst-case scenarios could include an attacker, a person who could have already slipped into the back of Kim's house while Theo and she had been out front. It could turn into a repeat of what'd happened to his family.

Kim was an assistant district attorney and, just like cops, that particular job often drew trouble and made enemies. Still, it seemed a stretch that someone after her would have sent a screaming woman onto her property in some ploy to draw her out into the open so she could be harmed. In case that was exactly what had happened, though, Theo waited until Kim ran out into the yard with him.

"Have you seen or heard anything else?" she asked, shoving her arms through the sleeves of her coat. She reached into her pocket and came up with a small flashlight.

He shook his head and started walking, making a beeline toward the barn. However, he also continued to keep watch around them. If the ploy was indeed to draw Kim out, his mere presence might stop an attack. Might.

"Come out so I can see you," Theo shouted. "If you're in some kind of danger, I can help."

Still nothing, but the owl let out more of those hoots, and this time it sounded like a warning. Owls did that, Theo knew. They were like watchdogs when someone encroached on their territory, and the owl was somewhere in the vicinity of the barn as well.

"Got any threats recently that you haven't reported?" Theo whispered to her.

When she didn't immediately answer with a no, it caught his attention, and he slowed his pace a little to give her a chance to fill him in.

"Not exactly a threat," she finally said, keeping her voice to a murmur. "Rowena Odell called me yesterday to tell me she was worried that Quill was going to do something bad before his trial. She didn't spell out what that bad thing might be and didn't have any evidence I could use to have Quill's bail revoked. I can't revoke bail on a woman's bad feeling."

Theo was very familiar with that case since Rowena and her husband, Quill, were his ex-wife's parents. Theo had also been the one who'd arrested Quill for the latest incident of domestic aggravated assault. Quill, who was a mean man and an even meaner drunk, had stabbed Rowena in the abdomen during an argument.

By sheer luck or some would say the grace of God, Rowena hadn't died from her injuries, and now that she'd recovered, she was worried that Quill might try to go after her again. Or somehow wiggle out of a trial that would likely result in a twenty-year sentence. Or more.

With Quill's hot temper, Theo wouldn't put it past the man to threaten the judge, jury and Kim during the trial, which could result in even more charges. That's what had happened during Quill's bond hearing, and it was the reason the man had spent three months in the county jail before finally being released. Now, he was awaiting trial, and unless there was some sort of delay, it would start in just four days. Both Quill and Rowena had to be getting desperate about the man's fate.

"I mentioned Rowena only because she might try to create some kind of evidence to get the bail revoked," Kim muttered.

Yes, Theo had already gone there. "I'll talk to Rowena tomorrow," he assured Kim.

But this didn't feel like something the woman would do. No, the years of abuse had left her worn down. Yeah, she would make sobbing, pleading phone calls, begging for Kim and the cops to make sure Quill didn't get another chance to try to hurt her, but she wouldn't come screaming onto Kim's property to draw her out so she could try to coerce her in some way.

On the other hand, Quill would absolutely do something like that now he was a free man.

Quill could maybe be using someone—maybe even Rowena if he'd managed to get his hands on her—as a lure with the intentions of doling out what he would see as payback to the assistant DA and the arresting officer. But Rowena had been diligent about calling 9-1-1 if anyone even approached her house since she was afraid of Quill. That didn't mean, though, that the man hadn't managed to get to her, and that's why Theo fired off a quick text to Dispatch for someone to check on Rowena.

When Theo reached the corral gate, he stopped and listened to make sure they weren't about to be ambushed. Again, he heard nothing, not even the gate when he opened it. Obviously, Kim kept it well oiled. Too bad about that since a squeaky gate would have alerted him that the screaming visitor, or someone else, had gone through the corral and into the barn.

Of course, that visitor could have just scaled the wooden fence, and that's why Theo took hold of Kim's hand to aim the flashlight on the ground. In hindsight, he should have just instructed her to do it because touching Kim was akin to playing with fire.

He fanned the light over the corral and got a motherlode of an adrenaline punch when he saw the footprints. Not from shoes. But rather from bare feet.

Hell.

That had him moving faster, and with Kim right next to him, Theo hurried to the barn doors. Too bad Kim hadn't left a light on because the place was pitch-black.

"Hello?" Theo called out. "If you need help—"

He stopped when he heard the sound behind them. A crack as if someone had stepped on a twig, and he whirled around, moving in front of Kim. In the same motion, he brought up his gun. Not aiming at anything, just making it ready.

"Who's there?" Theo demanded, not expecting an answer.

He didn't get one either. However, he did hear some

rustling around in the trees to the right. Maybe an animal, but Theo's gut told him the sound was coming from a person. It was possible the barefooted visitor had changed her mind about going in the barn and had headed for the woods.

"I can help," Theo repeated, wishing he didn't always sound like a cop.

"I can help, too," Kim added. Obviously, she'd heard his tone and had decided a terrified woman wasn't likely to take him up on his offer.

They stood there, waiting. Listening. And even over the whipping of the wind, Theo heard the moan. Not coming from the woods but rather the barn. That got him moving again, but he kept Kim behind him when he stepped inside.

One of the horses had indeed sought out the warmth of the barn, and the gray mare whickered and flicked her tail. Theo had no trouble seeing her, but there were plenty of dark shadows caused by the stalls, hay and equipment.

Keeping his gun ready, Theo reached out and switched on the overhead light. Such that it was. The dim, bare bulb flickered on, and he immediately swept his gaze from one side of the barn to the other.

And he saw her.

A woman—and yes, she was barefooted—huddled by some bales of hay. She was sitting on the barn floor, her arms locked around her knees that she'd pulled up to her chest, and she was rocking back and forth. This definitely wasn't Rowena.

Theo didn't see any blood or other obvious injuries,

but he decided to go ahead and call Dispatch to ask for an ambulance.

"Are you hurt?" Theo asked after he'd made the call and put his phone back in his pocket.

Her head snapped up, her attention zooming straight to him, but he couldn't actually see her face that well because of the strands of her dark hair covering it. Making a small, feral sound, she scrambled back, deep into the corner, and huddled there.

"I'm the sheriff," he said, going a few steps closer. "I can help."

The woman didn't answer, but her gaze fired toward Kim when she moved. "It's cold in here," Kim murmured. She took a horse blanket that'd been draped over one of the stalls and went toward her.

The woman turned her head away, obviously trying to squeeze herself even tighter into the corner. Kim eased the blanket over her and stepped back.

"Who are you?" Kim asked, using that same gentle tone. "What can we do to help you?"

Those were both good questions, and once he had answers to them, Theo could hope she'd tell them why she was there and, better yet, who was she running from? Because it was obvious she was terrified. That terror might go up significantly when she heard the ambulance, so Theo angled himself in the doorway of the barn in case she tried to bolt.

Even though he could only see the side of her face, he tried to sort through her features to see if he recognized her. He didn't. She definitely wasn't a resident of Silver Creek. Of course, she could have been visiting someone. If she'd driven here, though, and her vehicle had broken down, that didn't explain why she wasn't wearing any shoes.

"You need to see a doctor," he said, going for the same soothing tone that Kim had used.

But it did just the opposite. The woman whirled toward him, and she frantically shook her head. "No," she said, her voice a rusty whisper. "He'll find me."

Theo latched right onto that. "*He*?" he pressed.

The woman opened her mouth but didn't answer. That's because she no doubt heard the sound outside the barn. Not the ambulance. No. This was the sound of running footsteps.

A hoarse sob tore from her throat and she went back into "hide and cower" mode. Kim sure didn't though. Theo realized it shouldn't have surprised him when Kim whipped out a snub-nosed .38 from her coat pocket. She was the daughter of a retired cop, after all, and had come face-to-face with violence. Of course, she'd grabbed her gun before coming out into the yard with him.

"Stay here with her," Theo instructed Kim even though he hated the notion of using her as backup. Still, he'd soon have real support when one of the deputies arrived with the ambulance.

Theo gave another sweeping glance around the barn to make sure this wasn't some sort of two-pronged attack with someone else already hiding inside. But he saw nothing. He didn't hear anything else either since the running footsteps had stopped.

"I'm Sheriff Sheldon," Theo called out to cover all the legal bases in case this turned into a gunfight.

Theo waited, listening, and he didn't have to listen very long before he heard the rustling sound on the side of the barn. He motioned for Kim to get down and stepped into the doorway where the wind gave him another slam.

Whoever had done that running wasn't anywhere in sight. No surprise there. With the few pieces of this puzzle that he had, it was most likely that the person out there was responsible for terrorizing the woman in the barn and wouldn't have wanted an encounter with the local sheriff.

Keeping watch around him, Theo took a few slow, cautious steps outside, and when he didn't spot anyone about to ambush him, he went to his right where he'd heard the last of those footsteps. He inched his way to the corner of the barn, raised his gun to a shooting position and took a quick look before he ducked back.

Still nothing.

In the distance, Theo heard the wail of the ambulance siren and figured it would be less than two minutes before it arrived. He had no doubts that a Silver Creek cruiser would be right behind it. Hell, maybe even some Rylands, too, if they'd gotten the word that an ambulance had been called to Kim's.

"Last chance to show yourself," Theo warned in a growl.

Whoever was out there must have heard him because there was more movement. More footsteps. Theo leaned out again from cover and caught just a glimpse of the shadowy figure running away. The person was dressed in dark clothes and was moving so fast that he or she was hardly a blur.

"Stop!" Theo yelled.

He considered firing a warning shot but dismissed it because he didn't want the bullet hitting one of Kim's horses or ricocheting off something and slamming into the barn. However, he did text for more backup because he intended to order a thorough search of the property.

He continued to wait, continued to watch, while the ambulance squealed to a stop in front of Kim's house. Two EMTs barreled out of the vehicle. Theo called out to them, motioning for them to head to the barn. As expected, the cruiser came to a stop, too, and Deputy Ava Lawson hurried out.

Theo had more than a dozen deputies, and Ava was as good as they came. He could turn this search over to her and deal with getting those much-needed answers from the woman.

"Jesse's on the way," Ava relayed, referring to Deputy Jesse Ryland, who was Kim's cousin along with being another good cop. "Is Kim hurt?"

Theo quickly shook his head, wanting to rid Ava of that particular worry because Kim and Ava were friends. "A woman showed up. A stranger," he clarified. "And I need the EMTs to check her out and then take her to the hospital."

Ava took a moment, obviously processing that. "You need a CSI team?"

"Not yet. We're looking for an unidentified person last seen there." He pointed to the dark woods. "Once

Jesse arrives, arrange a search. Consider this unidentified person armed and dangerous."

Ava gave a crisp nod and, while she kept watch, she took out her phone to set up that search. Theo went back into the barn to see the EMTs trying to examine the woman.

Trying.

It was hard to do that, though, with her scrambling away from them and making a sound like a wounded animal.

"It's okay," Kim said, moving in front of the EMTs. She stooped down so she'd be at eye level with the woman. "No one's going to hurt you. We just want to help you."

That brought on another round of frantic headshaking from the woman. "No," she whimpered. "Please no."

"All right," Kim murmured, moving in a little closer. "Can you tell us your name? I'm Kim Ryland," she tacked on when the woman didn't respond.

But that got a response from her. The woman's eyes widened and her mouth dropped open as her gaze combed over Kim. "Kim Ryland," she repeated in that hoarse whisper.

Theo didn't miss the recognition in the woman's voice, and he used that as he went closer to her. "You know Kim?" he asked.

Her attention shifted to Theo and, with a fresh wave of panic on her face, she started scrambling away again.

"It's okay," he said, repeating Kim's attempt. "I'm Sheriff Theo Sheldon. Kim and I can help you. These EMTs can help you."

The woman went completely still. So still that he got a really bad feeling in the pit of his stomach.

"Theo?" the woman muttered. "Kim?"

"Yes," he confirmed, taking a step closer to her. "Do you know us?"

She nodded, and tears began to water her eyes. "I know you," the woman verified. "Help me, Theo. Please help me." A sob tore from her mouth and her eyes rolled back in her head as she was quickly losing consciousness. "It's me, Faith. I'm your sister."

Chapter Three

I'm your sister.

Those words continued to repeat in Kim's head as she paced the waiting room of the Silver Creek Hospital. They had been the woman's last words before she had passed out.

Faith's words.

Well, maybe.

Even though the EMTs had whisked the woman into the ambulance to take her to the hospital, Kim had fixed her face in her mind. Not only her features but also the sound of her voice. Along with mentally repeating the words, Kim was trying to figure out if there was anything familiar about the woman who'd spoken them. Anything to confirm that this was indeed her childhood friend who'd disappeared twenty-one years ago.

Theo was obviously trying to do the same thing. He, too, was pacing while he was on the phone. Kim didn't know specifically who he was talking to on this particular call, but he was arranging for a fingerprint kit and DNA test to be delivered ASAP.

The fingerprint kit would be especially helpful since

Faith's prints had been retrieved from several of her toys and had been placed in the various databases. In the early days after she'd gone missing, the optimism had been high that she would be found, but as the years had passed and been filled with false sightings, that optimism had dimmed considerably. Kim was keeping her "this isn't Faith" mindset for now because she didn't want to get up her hopes only to have them crushed again.

Before Theo's call about the fingerprints and DNA, he'd first arranged for a deputy to stay with Nadia and Jack. Just a precaution, Theo had said, but Kim had seen the concern in his eyes. Since they didn't know who or what they were dealing with, it was best that his son and Nadia be protected.

Kim pivoted toward the ER doors when they swished open and she saw her parents, Darcy and Nate, hurry in. She hadn't called them yet, but it didn't surprise her that they'd heard the news. By now, the buzz about what had happened was probably all over Silver Creek, and this particular bombshell would pack a much bigger punch than her merely having received another of those mystery letters.

"Are you all right?" Darcy asked, going straight to her and pulling Kim into her arms.

Darcy, the woman who'd been her mom since Kim was three. Her bio mom had died when Kim had been just a baby, and when her dad had married Darcy, Kim had gained a brother, Noah, who was now a San Antonio cop. Their younger brother, Hayden, was a marshal.

"I'm okay. Not sure about Theo, though," Kim added in a murmur when she glanced over at him.

The concern on Nate's face went up another level. With reason. To her father, Theo was family now since Grayson and his wife had raised Theo at the Ryland ranch after Theo's parents had been murdered.

He also gave Kim a hug the moment Darcy eased back. "Is it really Faith?" her father asked.

"To be determined." Rather than go over everything, Kim started with a simple question. "How much do you know about what happened tonight?"

"Theo updated Grayson, and I got the basics from him," her father explained. "You received another letter, called Theo to come over and then this woman showed up. Theo also spotted someone near the barn, but the person ran off before Theo could get a good look at him."

Kim nodded and appreciated the bottom-line approach. Her dad knew full well that she was an emotional wreck right at the moment, but he was keeping her focused on the specific elements of what was now a police investigation. Because, as he liked to say, *Sometimes the devil was in those details*. Kim might unknowingly have more details to make this picture a whole lot clearer.

"I haven't noticed anyone hanging around my place," Kim volunteered. "I've had no concerns that anyone was watching or following me. No odd phone calls. Well, none that weren't connected to Rowena and Quill Odell," she added, speaking of the troubling case she was prosecuting. A case that both her parents were well aware of.

"Grayson asked Theo if the guy he saw was Quill," her dad volunteered. "But Theo couldn't be sure."

Of course, Grayson had asked that. Everyone in her family knew that Quill was basically a bully and that he might stoop to intimidation tactics what with the aggravated assault charges looming over him. But it seemed an unlikely coincidence that Quill would have showed up the same night as the woman.

Kim turned again when she heard the footsteps behind her, and she saw Theo making his way toward them.

"Just got an update from the doctor," Theo said. He tipped his head in greeting to her parents. "The woman's injuries don't appear to be serious, but she does have some cuts on her feet and hands."

The woman. Not said with a ton of emotion but more like a cop's briefing. Kim totally got that. It was best not to jump right into the scalding memories of the past until they knew what they were dealing with.

"Sometime over the past couple of hours, she also received an injury to her head," Theo went on. He tapped the back of his own head to show them the location. "Could be blunt force trauma, or it could have happened during a fall."

Well, there would have been plenty of opportunities for a fall, what with her running across Kim's property, and heaven knew where she'd been running before that.

"She's conscious," Theo continued to explain, "and I'm about to go in and talk to her. I want you there for that," he added to Kim. "She seemed to settle down some when you talked to her. I want to keep her calm so we can figure out if she is who she's claiming to be."

Kim nodded. "You want me to question her?"

"No, but be ready to step in if she starts to get agitated. Dr. Sanchez probably won't give me much leeway with an interview if his patient is getting hysterical." Theo turned to Nate. "One of the deputies will be bringing over the fingerprint kit. Can you hang around and wait for that?"

"Will do," her father assured him.

Theo muttered a thanks and he put his hand on Kim's lower back to get her moving. A gesture that didn't last because he pulled away just as fast. They'd learned the hard way over the years that touching wasn't a good thing.

They were still a few steps away from the examination room when someone called out Theo's name. A very familiar voice belonging to Nadia Odell Sheldon, Theo's ex. She was wearing mint-green nurse's scrubs, and she came toward them at a brisk pace.

"I didn't know you had to work tonight," Theo immediately said to her.

"Ditto." Nadia turned her cool blue eyes to Kim. "Ditto," she repeated.

That short response bundled a frigid Texas-sized smackdown. Kim didn't think she was reading into it either. Nope. Nadia had made it clear that she believed Kim had had an affair with Theo. She hadn't, but nothing had been able to convince Nadia differently, and the woman had even cited that accusation when she'd filed for divorce.

"I got called in because we had two nurses who had to go home sick, and there were some emergencies," Nadia added. "Jack's with the nanny and Deputy Norris, who you sent over." She paused. "You said there wasn't a threat to Jack, that the deputy was there only as a precaution. I hope you're right. I wouldn't have come in if I'd thought Jack was in danger."

"He's not," Theo was quick to assure her. "But I'd like to keep a deputy in place for the next few hours. At least until we interview someone."

"The mystery woman you found at Kim's," Nadia remarked. So, the gossip had already started. Of course, Nadia was probably thinking that Theo had been at her place for something other than official business.

"I'll see you tomorrow when I pick up Jack," Theo added to Nadia.

He didn't hang around to give Nadia time to respond to that, but she kept her eyes on them while they went into the examination room. Theo shut the door and turned his attention to the woman on the bed.

There was no one else in the room, yet it was obvious the medical staff had been here. She had an IV in the back of her left hand, and some spots on her feet had been cleaned and bandaged.

Since there was plenty of light, Kim took a fresh look at the woman's face. She was indeed covered with small nicks, and there were bits of leaves and twigs in her long brown hair. Faith had had much lighter hair, like Theo's, but some people's hair did darken as they aged. Not to mention, it could be dyed.

The eyes were the right color. Blue that had lots of

gray in them. But Kim couldn't get her mind to do a mental age progression to see if Faith's childhood eyes and the rest of her features matched this one.

"Theo," the woman said.

Her voice hardly had any sound, but there was plenty of wariness in her eyes when her attention landed on his badge. She didn't try to scramble back as she'd done in the barn, but it was obvious she was uncomfortable being in the room with a lawman. Or maybe that discomfort extended to anyone and everyone right now because she didn't give Kim a welcoming look either.

"I need to know who you are and how you ended up here in Silver Creek," Theo said. He didn't go any closer. He continued to stare at her from the end of the bed.

The woman flinched as if he'd slapped her. "I'm Faith. Don't you remember me?"

Theo made a sound that could have meant anything. "My sister, Faith, went missing twenty-one years ago when she was eight."

"Twenty-one years," she repeated in a whisper. "So long." Her bottom lip began to tremble. "You don't remember me."

"If you remember me, why did it take you all this time to get in touch with me?" he countered.

She looked straight at him, but her eyes still looked a little unfocused. "Because I didn't know who I was. Because I only recently found out that I wasn't the person I believed I was."

Kim thought her time as an ADA had given her a decent gauge for detecting lies, and that sounded like the truth. But she wasn't about to believe anything until she had some more facts.

"Explain that," Theo insisted. "Why did it take you twenty-one years to find out?"

The breath she dragged in was long and slow. "Because people lied to me. Because the people I thought were my parents lied to me," she amended. She closed her eyes a moment as if trying to steady herself or fight off a dizzy spell. "Their names were Vicky and Clifton Neely, and they told me my name was Ashley."

Kim was seriously tempted to take out her phone and do a search on the people she had just named, but she didn't want to do something that might break the woman's attention. Soon though, Kim had no doubts that Theo and she would know everything about them.

Including whether or not they even existed.

Over the past couple of decades, three different women had showed up, claiming to be Faith. That'd happened shortly after the media had done stories on the anniversaries of the murders and Faith's disappearance. In all three cases, the claims had turned out to be false and motivated by money. Even though Theo hadn't touched a dime of it, his folks had left behind several million dollars in assets. Assets that might have been the original motive for the murders if the killer had come to the ranch hoping to find a large stash of cash. Apparently, there were those willing to go to great lengths, including pretending to be his sister, to get their greedy hands on the money.

"An eight-year-old would have known if the Neelys were actually her parents," Theo pointed out.

The woman shook her head. "I couldn't remember anything before age eight. They told me I'd been in an accident, that I'd fallen in a creek and had been hurt when I hit my head on a rock." She pushed back the hair on her forehead to reveal the thin white barely there scar, and then she paused. Her hand was trembling. "Sometimes, I'd get flashes of memories, but they always said I'd just dreamed it and that it wasn't real."

If all of this was true, then the Neelys—or whatever their real name was—had at best concealed a kidnapped child. At worst, they'd been killers and kidnappers. It seemed beyond extreme, though, to murder a couple just to steal a child they wanted to raise, but that's exactly what could have happened.

"What kind of flashes of memories did you get?" Theo asked.

The woman groaned softly, and her fingers twisted and tightened on the bit of sheet she'd latched onto. "Just of another house. Of toys. Of a boy and a girl. I think they were you," she said, glancing first at Theo and then at Kim. "But the memories didn't make sense, and I was always terrified of them."

Theo shifted, moving closer until he was practically looming over her. "Why did they scare you?"

"Because they didn't fit with anything that was in my life, but they were so real…" The woman stopped, shuddered and blinked hard as if she was fighting to concentrate. Or fighting to block out some images going through her head. "Sometimes, in the memories, I'd see blood on a wood floor."

There had indeed been blood, and the floor had been

wood. But Kim reminded herself that a detail like that was something the woman could have gotten from the news reports.

"I'll want to speak to your parents," Theo insisted.

She shook her head. "You can't. They died in a car accident two months ago." Once again, she stopped, and this time she swallowed hard. "That's when it started. That's when the memories or whatever they were started getting stronger. Memories of being carried out of a house in the dark. Of someone running with me. I was wearing pink pajamas, and I was crying and calling out for help."

Kim tried to keep her face blank, and she figured that Theo was attempting the same thing, but Faith had indeed been dressed like that when she'd disappeared. Kim was well aware of it since she'd had identical PJs and had been wearing them on that horrific night. Faith had also called out for help.

A reminder that Kim got every time someone sent her one of those letters.

Had this woman sent those letters? Maybe. But if so, it seemed a long time to stretch out a con.

"I started looking through my parents' things," the woman went on. "Through files and old photos, to see if there was anything. I found my birth certificate. Or what I thought was mine, but I started doing some searches on the internet and I learned that my parents...that the Neelys had a daughter named Ashley who'd drowned when she was seven."

Kim glanced at Theo to see if he had a take on that. He didn't. Well, not a visible one anyway, but he was probably thinking that if this woman was lying, then she'd done her homework. The details of a drowned daughter would fit right into a couple desperate for a child. A child they might have been willing to get through any means they considered necessary. Including kidnapping and murder.

"How did you come to believe that you might be Faith Sheldon?" Kim asked her.

"More internet searches," she readily answered. "I just kept digging, looking for a child who would have been adopted or gone missing about twenty-one years ago. I thought maybe my parents had found me, hurt and maybe wandering around without my memory, and they decided to keep me."

That was a possibility, too, but most people would have reported finding a child. Well, they would have unless they had believed the girl would be in danger if they turned her over to the authorities. Yes, she really did need to do some digging into the Neelys.

"I found some articles about the couple who'd been murdered and their missing daughter," the woman went on, lifting her eyes to Theo. "I saw a picture of you. You were twelve or so, and you were the boy from those flashes of memory that I'd been getting."

The silence filled the room, corner to corner, and for several long moments, the only sound was the soft beep of one of the machines.

"You don't believe me," she said, her voice cracking and then fading to no sound whatsoever when she repeated the words like a mantra.

No way was Kim immune to the raw emotion she

heard, but she couldn't let herself give in to it. Theo obviously didn't either.

"So, how'd you get to Silver Creek?" he asked.

The woman closed her eyes, a single tear spilling down her right cheek. "I'm not sure. I, uh, must have had a blackout or something."

Theo huffed, clearly frustrated with these answers. "What's the last thing you recall before the blackout?"

She certainly didn't jump to respond. She touched her fingers to her head, shook it. "I was in San Antonio. The next thing I remember is the two of you coming into the barn."

"The barn where you'd run. And where you were hiding," Theo pointed out. "Why? Who or what were you afraid of?"

She shook her head again and this time it wasn't just a single tear that slid from her eye. She made another of those hoarse sobs and began to cry.

There was a brusque knock at the door, and when it opened and Dr. Sanchez came in, Kim figured he'd heard the crying, too. The doctor scalded them both with a warning glance to let them know he wasn't pleased about their upsetting his patient, and he hitched his thumb in the direction of the waiting room.

"You've got a visitor," the doctor said to Theo. "He's insisting on talking to you right now. Says it's important, that it's about my patient."

Until he'd added that last part, Theo had made no move to leave, but that had him muttering, "I'll be right back," and he headed into the waiting room.

Kim went with him, and she spotted the lanky man

with salt-and-pepper hair wearing jeans and a plain white shirt. His face was etched with concern.

"Sheriff Sheldon." The man made an immediate bee-line toward them. "Is Ashley Neely in that room? Is she hurt?"

Theo put out his hand to stop the man from charging past him and into the room. "Who are you?"

"Greg Conner," he snapped, clearly not happy with being stopped. His attention stayed pinned to the ex-amination room door. "If Ashley's in there, I need to see her."

"And why is that?" Theo was in the "full cop" mode now.

Greg shifted his attention to Theo, and his dust-gray eyes narrowed. "Because she's my fiancée. And because she needs help."

"She's getting help," Theo assured him. "You said her name is Ashley Neely?"

It was a simple question, but apparently the answer wasn't as simple because Greg muttered some profanity under his breath. "She told you she was Faith Sheldon," he finally said. "She's not."

Kim couldn't bite back the groan. Not another hoax. Yes, she'd sworn she wouldn't get up her hopes, but that had happened anyway. Kim had started to believe that this might indeed be the childhood friend she thought she'd lost forever.

"Then why would she believe she is Faith Sheldon?" Theo countered.

Again, Greg was slow to answer, and the sigh he made was heavy and long. "Because my fiancée isn't well. In fact, she escaped in the early hours of the morning two days ago so she could come here to Silver Creek and go through with this farce of being your long-lost sister."

"Escaped?" Theo and Kim asked in unison.

Greg nodded and scrubbed his hand over his face. "Yes, for the past two months, Ashley has been confined to a psychiatric hospital."

Chapter Four

Theo had no trouble hearing what Greg had just said. That the woman claiming to be Faith had escaped from a psychiatric hospital. Maybe it was true. In fact, maybe everything Greg was saying was the truth, but there was something about the man that set Theo's teeth on edge.

Because Theo's cop instinct told him that Greg wasn't being completely honest.

Theo took out his phone and sent a text to Deputy Ava Lawson to ask her to do a quick background check on Ashley Neely. Soon, he'd know if there had indeed been an escape. But he figured there had been. Greg probably wouldn't have told a lie that could be so easily disproved.

"Why does your fiancée believe she's my missing sister?" Theo asked Greg the moment he'd finished the text.

That caused Greg to dole out a weary sigh. "Because she read about your family being murdered. A lot of papers did articles about it last year on the twentieth anniversary. Ashley became obsessed with it and started to believe she was Faith. She isn't," he quickly added.

"You're sure?" Theo argued, but he should have been

asking himself a version of that since he wasn't sure one way or another who he was dealing with here.

"I'm sure enough," Greg answered. "I've known her a long time, and there's no proof whatsoever that she's anyone other than Ashley Neely." He added a firm nod to that. "I want to take her back to the hospital in San Antonio. You don't have a right to keep me from seeing her, from taking her."

Theo tapped his badge. "Yeah, I do. Right now, the woman in question needs medical attention."

"If her injuries aren't serious, I can have her moved back to the psychiatric hospital so she'll be with medical staff she knows," Greg pressed. There was both concern and worry in his voice and expression, but, once again, Theo got a bad feeling that the emotions weren't all genuine. "I need to see her."

Since it was possible that the woman would want to see Greg, as well, Theo didn't totally nix the idea of him seeing her. However, she wouldn't be leaving the hospital or Silver Creek until Theo had answers.

"This is assistant district attorney Kim Ryland," Theo said, tipping his head to Kim. "Were you on the grounds of her property in the past couple of hours?" he asked Greg.

Greg shifted his attention to Kim as if just remembering that she was standing there. "No. Why would I have been there? I don't even know her."

"You tell me," Theo pressed.

Annoyance flickered across the man's face. "No, I don't believe I was on her property because I have no idea where her place even is."

Maybe. But Theo was pretty sure that was a lie. If the man's fiancée truly believed she was Faith Sheldon, then Greg would have likely dug enough into the murders to know the key players. Kim was absolutely a key player because she had not only been on scene when Theo's parents had been killed, she'd also been Faith's best friend.

"Then why were you in Silver Creek?" Theo asked Greg.

Greg opened his mouth, closed it and obviously rethought what he'd been about to say. He gave a heavy sigh and restarted. "When Ashley went missing from the hospital two days ago, I hired a PI right away to look for her. He's been monitoring police reports, and he called me when he heard about the woman you found. A woman matching her description. I drove here right away because I was certain it was her."

Theo leveled his gaze on the man, hoping to make him uncomfortable or even pissed off. Because uncomfortable, angry people often said things they'd rather have kept to themselves. Greg, however, stayed quiet.

"I want the name of that PI," Theo insisted since it was possible the guy had broken the law in getting that info on the woman they'd found. "And you won't mind me checking your GPS or your phone to verify that you got the call from the PI and then drove here."

Oh, there came the anger. "I believe you'd need a warrant for that."

Bingo. There was something to hide. And that meant the man might be lying about everything.

"Wait here," Theo told Greg, and he made sure it

sounded like the cop's order that it was. "I'll have a word with the patient."

Theo didn't linger waiting for Greg to object, but he did motion for Kim to go with him. For one thing, now that she'd had some time to think about it, Kim might be able to see something in the woman's features to help confirm who she was or wasn't. Theo also didn't want to leave Kim alone with a man he wasn't sure he could trust.

"He's lying about something," Kim muttered to Theo once they had stepped back into the examination room.

Theo didn't smile, but it was nice to know they were on the same page. Then again, Kim and he usually were. That was the problem. Along with having like minds, there was the heat. Not a soft whisper of attraction either.

Nope.

This was the full-blown deal. Normally, Theo could just put it on the back burner by not being around her, but he didn't see that happening any time soon. He needed, and wanted, her on this particular investigation. Not solely because she could help, but also because he was concerned about her safety. If this was actually Faith lying in the bed, looking at them with hopeful but wary eyes, then it meant his parents' killer might also be nearby.

"I heard Greg's voice," the woman said, her words rushed together with her heavy breaths. "I don't want to see him."

That got Theo's attention. "He claims he's your fiancé. Most people would want to see the person they intend to marry."

She swallowed hard. "He wanted me to stay at the hospital in San Antonio, but I couldn't." She leaned in, as if telling a secret. "The killer was there. The person who killed our parents was there."

Everything inside Theo went still. "Who's the killer?"

The woman glanced away, shook her head. "I don't know. He stayed in the shadows, but I know it was him."

Theo took a moment to process that. "The killer kidnapped my sister the night he murdered my parents. If you are the person you're claiming to be, then you'd know who killed them and took you."

Her gaze slowly came back to him. There were tears in her eyes, and she turned them toward Kim. "You believe me, don't you? We were best friends. You were staying at my house." She sat up, her face brightening as if she'd just recalled something. "And you had a stuffed dog. A little brown and white one. We were sort of old for stuffed animals, but you'd brought it with you for the sleepover."

Kim kept the sound that she made noncommittal as she walked closer to the bed. "There was a photo of me with the dog. A picture that someone took before the cops could secure the scene. That picture made its way to the internet."

Kim was right about that. A teenage boy, Denny Travers, had been driving past the house just as Nate had carried Kim out. And she'd had the stuffed dog with her. Denny had used his phone to snap some pictures, including the one of Kim. He hadn't posted the photo right away but rather a few years later, and yes, plenty of people had no doubt seen it.

After the photo had gone public, Denny had been questioned. Or rather, grilled, and grilled hard because it'd riled the then sheriff Grayson to have his niece put back through an emotional wringer. Theo hadn't been a cop yet, so he hadn't been a part of those interrogations, but Grayson had finally concluded that Denny hadn't been part of the murders and kidnapping or that he hadn't seen anything that would help him identify the killer.

"Well?" Theo pressed when the possible imposter just stared at him with hurt in her eyes. "Did you see the picture of Kim with the stuffed dog or not?"

"No." Her voice had dropped to a whisper again. "I remembered that she had it." She looked at Kim. "You brought it with you. I swear, I'm not lying. It's an actual memory."

So, she was sticking to her story about being Faith. But if she was, why was her fiancé so sure that she wasn't? It was definitely something Theo intended to find out.

"What else do you remember?" Kim asked her. She kept her tone soft and level, and since she seemed to have a calming effect on the woman, Theo intended to let Kim keep up the questions.

On a heavy sigh, the woman dropped back against the pillow. "Not much. Only some pieces. I remember being carried out of the house, but I can't recall the person who did that. I remember Theo and you though. Not just from that night but little pieces of memories of us playing together."

"Do you remember where or what we were playing?" Kim continued.

The woman's forehead bunched up as if she was thinking hard to make the answer come. Theo knew what she could actually be doing was trying to come up with something that would sound believable.

"Once we were playing chase, or maybe hide-and-seek, in the yard," the woman finally said. "You and I were giggling when we ducked behind a tree. I think we were hiding from Theo."

The word that came to mind for Theo was "generic." Most kids had played chase or hide-and-seek, and if this woman had seen any photos of the ranch where Faith and he lived, she would know there were trees.

"You had a crush on Theo," she blurted, aiming that at Kim.

Well, that sure as heck wasn't generic. But then Theo frowned. It was possible this woman was picking up on the heat vibe between them. Equally possible, too, that she'd simply guessed.

"Is that true?" the woman asked Kim. "Did I get that right? You had a crush on Theo?"

Kim clearly wasn't comfortable with the question but she nodded. "You recall me telling you that?"

She shook her head. "It was more of a feeling I got because of the way you looked at him." She stopped and shifted her attention to Theo. "I suppose Greg told you I've been in the hospital?"

Theo was glad for the shift in topics. Not only because the crush talk was making both Kim and him uncomfortable but since this was definitely something he wanted to know about. "He did. He said you escaped from a psychiatric hospital."

The woman huffed. "I left. I wasn't confined there. I'd admitted myself voluntarily because... I was having some problems. Horrible dreams, flashbacks, and I was upset over the deaths of my adoptive parents." She paused again, and her bottom lip trembled.

"What kind of flashbacks?" Theo asked.

"Screams." The woman shivered. "I kept hearing screams and saw pools of blood. I'd hoped if I had intense therapy that I could figure out what was real and what wasn't."

Theo might be able to confirm some of what she was saying if he could get her permission to speak to her doctor. *Might*. It was likely, though, that her doctor would claim she wasn't in any mental state to give that permission.

Theo waited to see if she'd add more but when she didn't, he shifted the conversation in yet another direction. "Before they died, did you ever come out and ask your adoptive parents about your suspicions?"

Another nod, and she didn't hesitate either. "They said I was their daughter, that I wasn't Faith Sheldon, that I was having the dreams and flashbacks because I'd gotten too involved with the research I was doing about the murders."

Theo was about to press her to explain, but his phone dinged with a text from Ava.

Fingerprint kit is on the way to you. Will have more for you soon, but here's the preliminary on Ashley Neely. She's twenty-nine, a freelance data processor with an address in San Antonio. No criminal record. Her fiancé,

Greg Conner, filed a missing person's report on her nearly forty-eight hours ago.

That would have been about the time Greg had said Ashley had left the hospital. If she'd committed herself, the San Antonio cops must have decided there was a valid reason to be concerned as to her whereabouts. Then again, maybe Greg had put a spin on things to make it seem like Ashley was in danger.

That, she could be.

If his parents' killer truly believed she was Faith, then that person wouldn't want her to recall the details of that fateful night. The Neelys might not have wanted that, either, had they still been alive.

Theo thanked Ava for the preliminary and turned back to the woman in the bed. "How did the Neelys feel about you trying to recover memories of anything that happened before the accident they'd claimed you had?"

"They weren't in favor of it," she readily admitted. "They thought the best thing for me to do was go ahead and marry Greg and focus on that."

"They approved of Greg?" Kim jumped right in to ask.

"Yes." Her mouth tightened. "Greg and my parents were close friends. Greg's twenty years older than me, and they'd known him all his life."

Theo took a moment to decide how to best put this. It wouldn't be wise to start with an attack on the Neelys or Greg that might make the woman go on the defensive. "Since they were friends, your parents must have been pleased when you got engaged to Greg."

"They were pleased," she admitted. "And they weren't especially concerned that Greg was so much older than I am. They thought it was best for me to get married and have children. That it would make me feel more settled."

So, an old bond between Greg and the Neelys, and if Greg was twenty years older than Ashley, it would have made him twenty-eight at the time Theo's parents had been killed. Theo didn't want to build a theory on that just yet, but he had to at least consider that Greg had gotten Ashley for the Neelys. Maybe not by killing but by being associated with the killer.

Theo glanced at Kim to see if she was thinking the same thing. She must have been because she gave him a subtle nod. But for that theory to be true, it had to mean that Ashley was indeed Faith. It was time for him to push a little harder so he could try to find out if that was possible.

"Tell me the childhood memories you've been able to recall," Theo instructed her. "Not ones triggered from photos or what you've researched. Nothing vague, either, like hide-and-seek. Try to give me something specific."

He figured she'd have to take some time on that and might not even be able to come up with anything. Especially might not be able to do it if all of this was a fake. Or if she were delusional.

But she didn't take time. She didn't even hesitate.

"I remember Kim shrieking when you sneaked up on her and put an ice cube down her back. It was summer and very hot."

Theo didn't have to take any time either. Because he

recalled such an incident. Apparently, so did Kim because she gave him a knowing glance. A memory like that wouldn't have been on social media since they'd all been too young for that sort of thing then. Kim and Faith would have only been about six years old, and he would have been ten.

Theo would have definitely pressed for more such memories had the door not inched open. He immediately pivoted, stepping in front of the bed and placing his hand on the butt of his weapon. Kim moved to his side, and while she didn't draw a gun, she appeared ready to give him backup if needed.

Greg poked his head in. "Oh," he muttered when his attention landed on the position of Theo's hand.

"I told you to wait outside," Theo snarled.

"I know, but I just needed to see Ashley for myself. I have to make sure she's okay."

Theo turned so he could get a glimpse of the woman's reaction while also keeping an eye on Greg. It wasn't happiness he saw on her face. More like dread.

"It'll help to talk to me," Greg insisted, his gaze drilling into Ashley's. "You know it will."

Ashley gave a slight nod. Definitely not a convincing one. And it gave Theo another bad feeling. A feeling that maybe she was accustomed to doling out the reactions that Greg wanted. Then again, if what she'd said was true, she had gone against Greg when she'd checked herself into that hospital.

"I'll be able to take you home as soon as the doctor gives the okay," Greg added to her. "I just checked with one of the nurses, and he'll be in here in a few minutes. I could have you home in an hour or so."

Ashley didn't shake her head, didn't refuse, but her gaze flew to Theo, and he could almost hear her pleading with him to intercede. That, he would do. No way did he intend for her to leave, especially with Greg, until he had some proof about her identity. Added to that, it might not be safe for her to go back to her house. It especially might not be safe for her to be alone with Greg.

Theo's phone rang and he saw Ava's name on the screen. Probably an update on the background check, which he wanted. But he kept his attention on Greg while he took the call.

"You're going to want to get as many people out of there as possible right now," Ava immediately said the moment he answered. "We just got a report that someone's about to detonate a bomb in the hospital."

Chapter Five

Even though Theo hadn't put the call on speaker, Kim was standing right next to him so she had no trouble hearing what his deputy had just told him.

A bomb.

The chill rippled over her skin, and Kim felt herself go on autopilot. They had to get out of there now. Because the killer could be back to finish what he'd started twenty-one years ago.

She took hold of the woman's arm, helping her from the bed, while Theo practically pushed Greg out of the room. No doubt because Greg could have been the one who'd planted an explosive before he'd even made his way toward his fiancée's room.

If there was an explosive, that was.

Since she was the daughter of a cop, she could see this as a hoax. A dangerous one. Meant to get them running outside so they could be attacked.

Still, they had no choice but to move. The killer hadn't created a hoax when he'd murdered Theo's parents, and this could also be the real deal now.

"Both of you stay close to me," Theo instructed the

woman and Kim. He'd already drawn his gun, and he now pressed the speaker function on his phone so that Ava could fill him in on the details.

"An anonymous 9-1-1 call came in through Dispatch," Ava explained as they moved. Not quickly. The woman was obviously weak, and she sagged against Kim. Greg started to move in as if to help, but Theo waved him off and hooked his left hand around Ashley's waist. "I've already sent you backup, and I've contacted the bomb squad."

Backup. Thank God. Kim knew all the cops in Silver Creek, and she trusted each and every one of them with her life. Good thing because it was possible their lives were on the line right now.

"I can help," Greg snapped. "Ashley is my fiancée. I want to take her away from here. Obviously, you're not able to protect her."

Theo shot the man a glare. "Back off now, or I'll charge you with obstruction of justice and impeding a police officer."

Greg gave Theo a return glare, but he didn't reach for Ashley again and moved out of their paths as they headed for the ER doors.

They weren't the only ones evacuating. Clearly, word had gotten out that the place might be blown up, and the medical staff was already in the process of assisting any mobile patients toward the exits. No one was running or screaming, but the feeling of panic was so thick that Kim could practically see it.

Of course, the flashbacks came. *Of course.* Of that sick panic when she'd been eight. It occurred to her that all the players who'd been in on that nightmare could be here right now. Faith, Theo, her.

And the killer.

Mercy, the killer could be right here.

"You're breathing too fast," Theo murmured, and Kim realized he was talking to her.

He spared her a quick glance that was likely meant to be reassuring, but what reassured her most was that it stayed just a glance. Theo then pinned his attention to keeping watch, no doubt to make sure they weren't about to be attacked. That steadied Kim enough that she was able to do the same.

The doors swished open as they approached, the winter air slamming into them, and when they stepped outside, Theo paused for a few seconds to look around. Apparently, he didn't see anyone who could be a threat because he headed toward his cruiser.

Kim glanced around, too, including a quick look over her shoulder where she expected to see Greg trailing along behind them. But he wasn't there. In fact, he was nowhere in sight, and she had no idea if that was good or bad. She didn't believe, though, that they'd seen the last of him.

"Is the killer after me?" Ashley murmured. She was shivering from the cold, and her teeth were chattering. "Because he thinks I know who he is."

That was a possibility. A strong one. Well, it was if Ashley was actually Faith. Of course, even if she wasn't, the killer might believe she was indeed Theo's missing sister. If so, then Ashley could definitely be the reason for this bomb scare.

Kim heard the wail of sirens, the ripple of panicked chatter and shouted orders from the medical staff. Someone was sobbing.

They were still a good ten yards away from the cruiser when Kim heard another sound. One that sent her heart leaping to her throat.

A gunshot.

She was certain of it. Apparently, Theo was, as well, because, muttering some profanity, he pulled them to the ground behind a car.

"This is Sheriff Sheldon. Everyone get down," Theo shouted. "There's an active shooter."

"Someone's shooting at us?" Ashley cried out. In a panic, she would have scrambled away from them if Kim hadn't caught onto her and put her facedown on the ground.

"Don't get up," Kim insisted.

Just as there was another blast from a bullet.

This shot tore through the car windows and sent glass spewing over them. Kim protected Ashley and herself as best she could by covering their heads with her arms, but she knew that wasn't going to stop a bullet from killing them.

Crouching next to her, Theo made a quick call to Ava to let her know what was going on. What he didn't do was get down. With his gun ready, he stayed in a position so he could peer over the hood of the car.

"Is it the killer doing this?" Ashley asked. "Is it the man who took me when I was a kid?"

That definitely fell into the "to be determined" category. And later Kim would need the answers to both of those questions. For now, though, she just tried to tamp down the fear crawling through her and focus on helping Theo. She did that by containing Ashley and trying to keep watch around them.

A third shot slammed into the car and hit just above their heads. Kim hadn't needed confirmation that they were the targets, but that gave it to her anyway. Someone was trying to kill them and just might succeed. Might succeed when it came to collateral damage, too, if the bullets ricocheted and hit someone else. She hoped everyone who'd evacuated had taken cover.

"The shooter's on the roof of the hospital, and he's using a rifle," Theo muttered in between some ripe profanity. While keeping his gaze pinned there, he took out his phone and called someone. A deputy, no doubt. "Get someone on that roof now. Take plenty of backup with you and be careful."

Even over her own heavy pulse causing her head to throb, Kim knew what that meant. It could take a deputy minutes—long, crawling minutes—to get to the roof and put a stop to this. Plus, the gunman would no doubt be ready for that and would likely try to take out any cop who came up after him.

Ashley was crying now, her body shaking from the sobs. Probably from the cold, too. Kim was certainly freezing.

"The roof," Ashley muttered. "He has us in his sights."

Probably, which was a good reason to stay down. Theo kept his position, though, looking up and trying to pinpoint the exact spot of the shooter.

Kim had actually been up on the roof. There was a

sitting area with an awning, and she recalled going up there when she'd been a teenager after her father was injured in the line of duty. Not a serious wound, but she had gone there to get away from her family so they wouldn't see her break down and cry.

The shooter would have had no trouble gaining access to that roof area as it wasn't hard to figure out how to get there.

A fourth shot hit the car again, but this time, Theo didn't just duck down. He took aim at the roof and fired. Considering the distance and the fact the shooter had plenty of cover, it would be hard for Theo to actually shoot him, but he was probably hoping it would cause the gunman to back off.

Kim held her breath, praying it would do just that. Of course, that meant the shooter might turn and run now that he knew he could get a taste of his own medicine, but if that happened, maybe the deputies would be able to apprehend him. It could turn into a shootout, though, with plenty of people getting hurt. But that might happen anyway if the deputies couldn't put a stop to it.

She hoped they didn't have to kill whoever was doing this. Because a dead man wouldn't be able to give them the answers they needed.

Kim counted off the seconds in her head. The *silent* seconds where there were no more shots. There were other sounds, though, of running footsteps that she hoped belonged to law enforcement. More sobs and murmurs, too. Then she heard a very familiar voice.

Her uncle, Deputy Jesse Ryland.

"The shooter's not up here," Jesse shouted. "I need all exits covered."

That caused Theo to whip out his phone again and make a call. He also shifted, keeping watch around them, and it occurred to Kim that if the shooter was no longer on the roof, then he could have bolted down the stairs and be coming for them.

Kim hadn't thought it possible, but her fear skyrocketed further. The shooter had missed them while he'd been aiming from a distance. However, if he could get close, he might be able to finish what he'd started.

The seconds crawled by, turning into minutes with Theo standing guard. Kim had her gun with her in a slide holster in her jeans, but she didn't have a target in sight. As it was, she could only cower and try to keep Ashley alive.

Kim got another slam of fear when she heard approaching footsteps, but she soon heard something that had her exhaling with relief.

"He's nowhere in sight," Jesse said, his tone the same he would have used when cursing.

Theo did curse, but he didn't ease up on his vigilant watch. Maybe because he knew the shooter could be hiding in the crowd of those who'd evacuated.

"Get the bomb squad in here so we can get the building cleared," Theo instructed. "Warn them that the shooter could be hiding inside, so they'll need a deputy with them."

"Will do," Jesse assured him, and he came around the side of the car to look down at Kim. "What about them?" he asked Theo.

"Have an ambulance sent here. I want Ashley loaded in it, and you stay with her. Once the hospital is cleared and she's back inside, I want a guard on her at all times. No one goes into her room or speaks to her unless they have permission from me." Theo paused only long enough to gather his breath. "And get someone out to Nadia's right away."

Kim's head whipped up, her gaze firing to Theo. "You think the shooter could go there?"

Theo shook his head. "I can't risk it."

No, he couldn't, not with his two-year-old son there.

Jesse gave him another assurance and took out his phone to get started on the calls he needed to make.

Theo shifted his attention to Kim. "Are you okay?" he asked.

She wasn't. Kim's nerves were firing on all cylinders, but she nodded. No need to give Theo any more worries than he already had.

And he did have worries.

Regret and guilt, too. Because he would take the blame for Ashley, her and the others being in danger. No way was this his fault, but he would see this as his fault for not being able to prevent it.

"When Ashley is secured," Theo continued a moment later, "you and I will go to my office. I need to find Greg. Find the shooter, too, if he's not the one who was pulling the trigger. If Greg had fired those shots, he got to the roof awfully fast, but he could have maybe managed it."

Yes, finding the gunman was a must. But there was something else on their proverbial plate, and it was something Kim could help him speed along. She could find out if the woman cowering beneath her was Faith Sheldon. If so, Theo's long-lost sister had finally made her way home.

And she'd brought a killer with her.

THEO STARTED RECEIVING updates from his deputies while he got Kim settled into his office. A familiar place for her since it was where her uncle Grayson had worked when he'd been the Silver Creek sheriff. He was hoping that familiarity and keeping her busy would soon settle her nerves.

His own nerves needed some settling as well. The shooter had fired four shots into a parking lot jammed with folks who'd evacuated from the hospital. They'd been damn lucky that there'd been no serious injuries.

And that's why he had to catch the SOB who'd pulled the trigger.

So far, there was no sign of him. No sign of Greg either. But there was a security camera on the ER doors and the footage could be analyzed. Theo would work on that once he was certain Kim was okay. She'd already briefly spoken to her parents, to assure them she was all right, but that was one of those kid-necessity deals. Theo had already done the same with a quick call to Grayson and Eve, and by now the Ryland clan had no doubt sprung into action.

Those with reserve deputy status, Mason, Gage, Dade and Kade, would already be assisting in any way they could. Some would almost certainly be at the hospital, trying to sift through the crime scene while making sure everyone was safe. One or two might also be at Kim's to assist the CSI team there. Any one of them would have also offered bodyguard duty to Jack. Theo might not have been born a Ryland, but he'd never doubted for a second that he was part of their family.

To give both Kim and himself a minute, he closed his door and looked her over to make sure there were no scrapes or cuts from when she'd landed on the concrete with Ashley. He didn't see anything other than a smudge of dirt on her cheek, and he automatically rubbed his thumb over it.

She flinched a little, no doubt because she'd trained her body to resist him. Especially resist any touching. Because, in the past, being so close to him had triggered flashbacks and even a panic attack. But she didn't back away this time.

With his fingers still on her cheek, Kim stood there, their gazes connected while the heat came. Stirred. And actually helped. The heat reminded him that she was alive. Safe.

Here.

And at the moment, that was the best he could hope for.

"Thank you," she said, not naming anything specific, and then she finally stepped back. Not far. And she fluttered her hands to his desktop computer. "Jesse should have taken and loaded Ashley's fingerprints by now. While you deal with the aftermath of the shooting and the bomb squad, I can see if the prints are a match to Faith's."

That was indeed a critical step in all of this and, either way, the news would be hard. If she wasn't Faith, then he'd have to deal with another imposter. Another gut punch over the crushed hope. But, if by some miracle, she was his sister, then he'd have to deal with that as well.

Along with the fact that someone wanted her dead.

Perhaps wanted Kim and him dead, too. Right now, there were too many unknowns, and the prints were a start.

He nodded, motioned for her to take his desk, knowing that she'd know how to work her way through the fingerprint database. She took off her coat, draping it over the back of the chair, and got to work.

Theo also took off his coat before he went to the laptop he kept on the corner of his desk. While he waited for his computer to boot up, he made his first call to Jesse, who told him the hospital had been cleared, that Ashley was secured in a room and that he'd called in a reserve deputy to guard her door. The reserve deputy was not only to make sure no one got in but that Ashley didn't try to leave. Theo doubted she would. That said, she had admitted she'd left the hospital in San Antonio, so it was possible she might try to do the same here.

With that base covered, Theo went to his next call. To Ava this time. But the deputy didn't have good news about the shooter. No sign of him. Thankfully, there had been no sign of a bomb either. Ava was going to remain at the hospital to help process the roof and the parking lot. If they could find spent shell casings, it could help them identify the type of gun used. Maybe even the shooter if he'd left prints on any of those casings. Though Theo figured that was a long shot.

After he'd made some other calls to the CSIs and to arrange for more reserve deputies to be brought in, he started the background checks on Greg and the Neelys while he glanced through the data that had come in on Ashley. He didn't see any immediate red flags, but he'd need to do a more thorough interview with her after he'd gathered as much info as possible.

He got an immediate red flag on Greg, though, when he saw the man had been taken to court over some unpaid debts. There was a current court order directing him to repay a lender ten grand.

"Greg's got money problems," he relayed to Kim.

She looked up, her gaze colliding with his. "Money problems that could be fixed if he marries Ashley?"

That's exactly where Theo's thoughts had gone. "Maybe. She's not hurting for funds. The Neelys left her an inheritance of nearly a million dollars."

Plenty enough money to fix Greg's legal problems, which might explain why he was pressing so hard to get Ashley to go with him. However, that wouldn't give him a motive for killing her. Well, it wouldn't unless she'd named Greg as her beneficiary in her will. That was something Theo needed to check.

"Jesse already loaded the fingerprints," Kim told him after a heavy sigh, "but the system is having trouble locating Faith's prints."

"'Trouble,'" he repeated, not liking what immediately came to mind. "As in maybe someone tampered with them?"

"No, it's more of a compatibility issue," she quickly answered. "Faith's prints were submitted in an older electronic format so a tech will have to go in and do a manual match. It might take a while."

"Hell," he grumbled. He was hoping he'd have an answer right away.

"I can go through reports as they come in from the deputies or the CSIs," Kim said, her forehead bunching up. She paused, muttered something he didn't catch. "Please give me something to do. I don't want to just sit here and think about how close we came to dying."

Theo mentally repeated his "hell." There was plenty he could give her to do—including checking social media for Greg, Ashley and the Neelys—but he doubted it was going to erase the worry he saw in her eyes. Nothing was going to erase it for him either. And that's why he did something reckless.

He pulled Kim to her feet and then into his arms.

They landed body to body and, mercy, every part of him was well aware of that. This hug might be for comfort, but it was impossible for him not to feel other things. Judging from the slight silky hitch of her breath, she was feeling them as well.

"I would say this was a bad idea if it didn't feel so good," she murmured.

Yep. He was in complete agreement with her. Theo didn't push things though. He definitely didn't put his mouth against her cheek even though that was what he wanted to do. However, he did draw in her scent, which, of course, gave him another hit of heat.

They stayed there, pressed against each other, with

his breathing picking up the rhythm of hers. That helped, too. Because it felt like they were together on even that most basic level. Along with the heat, he could feel his nerves leveling off. Could feel some of the tightness ease up in his muscles.

It didn't last.

The door opened and they flew away from each other as if they'd just been caught in the act of doing something very wrong. And, judging from the expression of the woman who froze in the doorway, they'd committed a whole host of wrongs.

Nadia.

His ex's mouth tightened. Her eyes narrowed, and Theo steeled himself for the onslaught. Oh, and it came all right.

"This is a sheriff's office," Nadia said, her voice snapping like a bullwhip. "There has to be rules or laws against this sort of thing."

"Theo was just giving me a hug because I was so upset," Kim blurted, obviously trying to defuse Nadia's anger. "Nothing else happened."

Of course, Nadia didn't believe that. Never had. She'd always thought Kim and he had had a raging affair. In Theo's mind, they had, so that's why he didn't even try to defend himself. Nadia could no doubt see what he felt for the woman he'd spent a lifetime keeping at arm's length.

"Is something wrong with Jack?" Theo asked Nadia, not just to shift the conversation, but because it was an immediate concern for him. "There's supposed to be a deputy with Jack and you."

Nadia didn't jump to respond, probably because she wanted to hurl more accusations or hang on to her anger since she was spoiling for a fight. But Theo just kept his calm stare on her.

"Jack's fine," Nadia finally said. "He's still with Deputy Norris and the nanny. The house is all locked up, and the security system is set."

Theo was glad those security measures were in place, but he would have preferred having Nadia tucked away with Jack instead of coming into town when a gunman was still at large. Deputy Roger Norris had plenty of experience in protection detail since he'd once been a marshal. Still, Norris couldn't help keep Nadia safe if she didn't stay put.

"I'm here because I got a call from Rowena," Nadia explained. Rowena, not *my mother*. Theo wasn't surprised by that since Nadia wasn't close to either of her parents. "She was upset and crying. Quill called to tell her he was on his way to her place to talk to her."

Theo groaned. "Did that SOB threaten to hurt her again?"

Nadia shook her head. "He didn't hurt her because he didn't show up." She paused and a fresh wave of concern took over her expression. "Look, I'm just going to come out and say it. I think Quill is the one who fired those shots at Kim and you."

Chapter Six

Kim had already geared up to try to assure Nadia that nothing was going on between Theo and her. No way did she want his ex playing dirty and maybe trying to keep Jack from him. But any assurances she'd planned fell away after she heard what Nadia had just said.

"You believe Quill tried to kill us?" Kim asked.

Nadia didn't jump to confirm her accusation. "I think it's possible," the woman finally admitted. She glanced over her shoulder and then her attention turned not to Kim but to Theo. "I don't want to be here when Rowena arrives, and I know she's on her way. Listen to what she has to say and then decide for yourself if Quill might have gone off the deep end and is going after the two of you."

Kim very much wanted to hear what Rowena intended to tell them, but she wanted more from Nadia. Dealing with Rowena wasn't always an easy task, and despite Nadia's wrong assumption about Theo and her having an affair, Nadia might have some correct info that could help them see the big picture here.

"What exactly has Quill done?" Kim pressed.

That caused Nadia to give an impatient huff and she shifted her purse in such a way to indicate she was leaving. "Quill is playing some kind of mind games with Rowena and I know he's very angry at Theo and you for his arrest and upcoming trial. Just talk to Rowena and then Quill instead of getting anything second-hand from me. It's hearsay. Isn't that a term you lawyers like to bandy about when something won't be admissible for trial?" she added with more than a hint of snark. "I have to go."

Nadia turned and walked out. Kim watched her leave before she turned to Theo. But Theo was already taking out his phone, and she saw him press Quill's number. Even though he didn't put it on speaker, she heard the call go straight to voice mail.

"This is Sheriff Sheldon," Theo snarled as he left a message. "I need you to come into the sheriff's office right away. If I haven't heard from you in an hour, I'll put out an APB and have you arrested and brought in."

Maybe Quill would comply, not because of Theo's threat but because any wrongdoing at this point could land him back in jail. With his trial less than a week away, even a short jail stay could play into the outcome of the verdict.

"I'm so sorry," Kim said once he'd finished leaving the voice mail.

Theo slowly lifted his gaze and leveled his eyes on her. "Please don't tell me you're apologizing because I hugged you. That hug was intended to comfort you after someone tried to kill you."

She gave him a level look right back. "I'm apologizing because of Nadia walking in on that hug." No way could she say she hadn't needed it and that it hadn't helped. It had. "I don't want her to give you any hassles about seeing Jack."

He sighed. "The terms of custody and visitation are all spelled out. What she can't spell out is who I hug." He paused a heartbeat and his gaze dropped to her mouth. He didn't say "or kiss," but she could tell that's exactly what he wanted to do.

And, oh, Kim wanted that as well.

The spent adrenaline and nerves were clearly playing into this, but she didn't need those things to feel the heat for Theo. Nope. Didn't need them and had no idea how to cool them down. It seemed as if they'd knocked over some old barriers, and she wasn't sure she could build them back up fast enough to stop this firestorm that was happening between them.

Kim didn't have time to give that more thought, or worry, because she heard the voices in the squad room, and she looked out, expecting to see Rowena. It wasn't. It was Greg, and he wasn't alone. He was with a beefy gray-haired man wearing a suit.

"I understand you've been looking for me," Greg said, his attention skirting right past Kim to land on Theo. Every muscle in Greg's face was tight with anger. A contrast to the man next to him, who appeared calm.

"I have been," Theo assured him at the same moment the guy in the suit said, "I'm Duran Davidson, Greg's lawyer. We're here to secure the release of his fiancée."

"No," Theo said without any hesitation whatsoever.

"Ashley is in protective custody. You might not have heard, but someone tried to kill her."

"Oh, I heard," Greg shot back as he came closer. "I heard, and I'm blaming you for her nearly being killed. I told you she should be with me, and you didn't listen. And now I suppose you're going to say I had something to do with the shooting."

Again, Theo didn't hesitate. "Did you? Because you disappeared mighty fast shortly before those shots started."

Greg responded to that with an "if looks could kill" glare, and he no doubt would have launched into a venomous comeback if the lawyer hadn't stepped in front of him.

"My client is upset," Duran said, still using that calm voice. "His fiancée, the woman he loves, was nearly killed, and he hasn't been able to see her, to make sure she's all right."

Theo kept his own glare on Greg. "She's safe, and until I'm convinced you're not a threat, you won't be seeing her."

Duran gave Greg's arm a pat before the man could speak. "Rather than stand here and debate this, why don't we all sit down and talk." He turned to Kim. "I'm guessing you're Kim Ryland?"

"I am," she verified. "How did you know that?"

"Greg told me that you were Faith Sheldon's childhood friend, so I did a quick check on the drive from San Antonio. You were at the Sheldon home the night Faith was taken."

"And the night Faith and Theo's parents were murdered," she quickly tacked on.

Duran nodded. "Now, you believe the shooting might have had something to do with what happened over twenty years ago."

"Did it?" she asked, trying to keep her tone as even as his.

"I don't think so, but it's something we should discuss. May we sit?"

Theo pulled in a long breath, stepped back and motioned for them to come in. They did, and Duran shut the door behind them.

"Since what I'm about to say is speculation and might harm reputations, I'd rather this chat be kept private," Duran insisted.

"I'd rather it be legal," Theo countered. "And since you're here with him, I'll go ahead and Mirandize him."

That caused Greg to curse and toss out another glare, but Duran simply put his hand on his client's arm again and motioned for him to sit in the chair next to Theo's desk. Obviously, Duran had a rapport with Greg and was keeping him in check, but his client clearly had a temper.

"All right," Duran said the moment Theo had finished reading Greg his rights. "My client understands what you've just told him, and he's here to cooperate by answering any questions you might have. But we'd like a show of good faith by allowing him to speak to his fiancée."

Theo shook his head. "He's not speaking to her until

I'm positive he won't try to intimidate her or do anything that'll add to her already terrified state."

"Terrified because someone shot at her," Duran quickly qualified. "My client will be able to help soothe her. She needs to be returned to the hospital in San Antonio so she can get both the physical and mental medical attention she needs."

"That's to be determined if he can do any soothing whatsoever," Theo argued, and he spoke right over Greg's loud and profanity-laced objection. "I want your client to submit to a gunshot residue test. If he doesn't, I'll get a court order, and I'll hold him here so he doesn't have a chance to try to change his clothes or attempt to wash it off."

Theo knew that GSR didn't wash off easily, and Greg was indeed wearing the same clothes he'd had on earlier. But even if he was the shooter, if he'd used a rifle to fire those shots or had worn gloves, then there might not be any traceable GSR. She had no idea what Duran's legal background was, but if he'd been involved in any trials or charges that involved a shooting, he was likely well aware of it.

"My client submits," Duran said, and it seemed to Kim that he gave Greg a warning glance.

Theo didn't waste any time. He made a call to the head of the CSI team that was still at Kim's house and asked that someone come to the sheriff's office right away to do the test.

"She'll be here in ten minutes," Theo relayed while he put his phone away.

"And when you get back the negative results, and

they will be negative," Greg insisted, "then I'll be able to see Ashley."

"Again, to be determined," Theo fired back.

Kim was betting that visit wouldn't happen any time soon. Theo wouldn't want to allow Greg to have any undue influence over what Ashley might say.

"What needs to happen before my client can see his fiancée?" Duran came out and asked.

Theo didn't hesitate. "For starters, he'll need to tell me the truth about Ashley, about any part he might have had in the shooting, and if at any time he was anywhere near Kim Ryland's house."

"I've already told you I was never at her house," Greg snarled before Duran could respond. "And I didn't shoot at anyone, especially the woman I love. Ashley and I are getting married. I have no reason to want her harmed."

Maybe. But Kim could think of a couple of reasons. Perhaps Ashley was becoming aware of who she actually was. Or rather, who she thought she was. If she believed she was Faith, then she might want to go to the cops, and if so, that could get Greg arrested if he had any knowledge of the Neelys' wrongdoing. Or if he'd participated some way in kidnapping her all those years ago.

But there was another possibility that Kim had to consider. Ashley might have fallen out of love with Greg or changed her mind about marrying him. Knowing that Greg had a temper, that loss of love or potential breakup with him could have caused the man to snap.

"And the other part," Theo prompted. "What's the truth about Ashley?"

Greg didn't snarl out a response this time, and Duran paused to take in a deep breath. It was Duran who answered. "It's possible Ashley is Faith Sheldon."

The air in the room went still, but Kim saw the muscles in Theo's jaw turn to iron. "Explain why you just said that."

Duran obviously needed to take another of those long breaths. "I knew the Neelys very well and have known Greg for years. I can tell you that Vicky and Clifton were simply crushed over the death of their daughter, and they were thrilled when they managed to adopt Ashley."

"How'd they get her?" Theo quickly asked.

Duran shook his head. "I don't know. I didn't handle the adoption, and when I pressed them on it, they said it'd been a private arrangement." He sighed. "Yes, I know how that sounds, but I can't believe either Vicky or Clifton would have participated in any way in a double murder for the sake of getting a child."

They might if they were desperate and, from the sound of it, they had been. Desperate to ease the grief over losing their daughter.

"You honestly think Ashley could be Theo's sister?" Kim challenged.

"It's possible," Duran said after a long pause. Greg only shook his head. "You'll have tests done to see if she is," the lawyer added to Theo. It wasn't a question.

"Of course," Theo verified. "But if she's not a match, that still leaves me with a huge problem. Who would want to fire those shots at her?"

"Well, it sure as hell wasn't me," Greg insisted, the

anger rising up in him again. He got to his feet. "I want to see my fiancée. It's my right."

Theo huffed. "No, it's not your right. But if you're clear on the GSR test and everything both of you have just told me checks out, then I'll ask Ashley if she wants to talk to you."

Kim had no doubt that if a visit actually happened, then Ashley wouldn't be alone with the man. Theo would make sure a deputy was with her in case things turned ugly or if Greg tried to browbeat her into leaving with him.

There was a knock at the door and when Theo opened it, Kim saw Veronica Reyes, a county CSI. Behind her, there was another familiar face.

Rowena.

So, Nadia had been right about the woman coming in and, judging from her nervous expression, this would not be a pleasant visit. Then again, that was the norm for any encounters with Rowena. Unlike Greg and even Quill, she didn't have a temper. Just the opposite. With her history of abuse, the woman always seemed to be on the verge of completely falling apart, so you had to be careful with everything you said to her.

"Go ahead into the squad room with CSI Reyes," Theo instructed Greg and Duran. "Once the GSR test is completed, you can wait until I call you back in for the rest of the interview."

Greg clearly didn't like being dismissed, but Duran and he went out of the office and followed Reyes to one of the unoccupied deputies' desks. Theo then motioned for Rowena to come in.

"Look, I'm not trying to defend Quill or anything," Rowena immediately said. "Not after what he's done to me. But I think someone's trying to set Quill up."

Kim sighed. "Why do you think someone is trying to set him up?"

Rowena took out her phone, pulling up a picture. "This was left on my doorstep last night. I found it this morning."

Kim looked at the photo and saw what appeared to be a dead rat. And blood. From the looks of it, something or someone had bashed in the rodent's head. Maybe because it'd gotten caught in a trap.

"Someone left that dead thing there to scare me," Rowena continued, her words rushed together. "To make me think it was Quill."

Kim couldn't see the logic in that. "Perhaps Quill left it to try to intimidate you."

"He wouldn't do that," Rowena quickly insisted. "He doesn't use scare tactics. He prefers his fists."

Quill's style was definitely more in your face. A direct confrontation—sometimes with his fists. But Quill probably understood that anything direct could and would put him back behind bars. So, perhaps he'd taken to something like leaving a dead rat to try to coerce Rowena into not testifying against him.

It wouldn't matter though.

Yes, it would be good to have the woman's testimony, but there was more than enough physical evidence for the man to be convicted of the vicious attack.

"Anyway, it was there when I opened my door this morning," Rowena went on. "It was disgusting, and I didn't want it there, so I got out the hose and washed it away."

Theo groaned softly because by washing it away, Rowena had also destroyed any potential evidence.

"Why would you think someone is trying to set Quill up?" Theo asked.

Again, Rowena answered without hesitation. "Quill's made some enemies over the years." She looked back at Kim again. "For instance, you could have put the rat there to make Quill look even guiltier, and you could have done that to make sure you don't lose at the trial."

Kim sighed. "Even if I was so inclined to fabricate evidence, which I'm not, I haven't had time to do anything like that." She paused, looked Rowena straight in the eyes. "Quill could be getting desperate. This could be a way he's hoping to get you to back off at the trial."

Tears sprang to the woman's eyes and her bottom lip trembled. "You must think I'm mad. And sometimes it feels as if I am. I want Quill in jail. I want him punished, but it'll twist me into a thousand knots to get on that stand and tell everyone what he did to me. What I allowed him to do to me by staying with him all these years," she added in a murmur.

And there it was in a nutshell. The effect of the damage that Quill had managed to inflict.

"Do you believe you're in danger, that Quill will try to assault you again?" Theo straight-out asked the woman.

Rowena shrugged but then shook her head. "No. Quill knows that coming after me now could send him to jail for the rest of his life. And whoever left the dead rat just wanted to do it to make me think it was Quill. Maybe to get Quill in trouble."

There was another possibility. Perhaps Quill had persuaded one of his friends to leave the dead rat. If Quill got Rowena scared enough, she might ask that the charges be dropped against him. They wouldn't be. But Quill might be willing to do anything to stay a free man.

Kim exchanged a glance with Theo, and she saw that he wasn't buying the notion that Quill wouldn't hurt Rowena again. The man likely would if he had the chance. Kim wanted to make sure that chance didn't happen, though she figured that Quill would eventually serve his sentence and get out. She doubted Quill would just forget about Rowena and let the woman get on with her life.

"If you honestly believe someone left you a dead rat to set up Quill," Theo said, keeping his voice calm, "then you should try to install a camera so you can see who's doing it."

Rowena's eyes widened a little, and her expression seemed to brighten. "Yes, that's a good idea. I can record whoever's doing it."

Yes, and if it was Quill, and Rowena managed to capture it with the camera, then that could be used against Quill at the trial.

"Also, if anything like this happens again," Theo went on, "call me immediately. Don't wash anything away."

Rowena nodded. "I'll make sure to keep my doors locked, too."

Kim had hoped the woman was already doing that, but maybe now she'd take even more precautions.

"I need you to file a report about the rat," Theo explained to Rowena, and he motioned toward the lone deputy, Nelline Rucker, in the squad room. The others were obviously still tied up with the shooting at the hospital. Nelline stood, listening to what Theo was saying to Rowena. "You'll also need to show Deputy Rucker the photo you showed us so she can get a copy of it."

Rowena muttered a thanks and headed in the direction of the deputy just as Theo's phone rang. "It's the lab," he muttered as he answered. He put the call on speaker. "Sheriff Sheldon."

"Hi, Sheriff. This is Shelby Martinez. I worked out the compatibility problem with the fingerprints you wanted examined and was able to run them."

Kim dragged in her breath. Waited. But she wasn't sure what to hope for. She wanted answers, but she hadn't thought it would come this soon.

"They're a match," Shelby added a heartbeat later. "Ashley Neely's prints are a match to those we have on file for Faith Sheldon." She paused. "The woman is your sister."

Chapter Seven

Theo heard what the lab tech had just said, but it took a couple of long moments for it to sink in. It didn't sink in well.

Ashley was his missing sister. She was Faith.

He heard the strangled sound that Kim made, and he knew this was hitting her as hard as it was him. They'd both been there that god-awful night when Faith had been taken. The night that had changed their lives forever. But it had changed Faith's, too. She hadn't died, as Theo had feared. She had survived, and was back here in Silver Creek.

"Sheriff?" the tech asked. "Are you still there?"

Theo had to clear his throat before he could speak. "Yeah. Thanks for the info. Could you document the match and send me a copy? Also, has anyone else recently asked for a comparison of my sister's prints?"

"I'll check and get back to you." There was a hesitation in her voice as if she wanted to add something. Maybe some kind of congrats or good wishes. But the tech must have realized what a shock this was for him and only muttered a goodbye.

Theo hung up and then just stood there, trying to process everything. Apparently, Kim was doing the same because she didn't say anything for a long time.

"Are you okay?" she asked.

No, he wasn't. One look at her and he knew she wasn't either. Theo shut the door and pulled her into his arms. She didn't resist, not one little bit. Kim made a hoarse sob and dropped her head onto his shoulder.

"This changes everything," she muttered.

It did. He had his kid sister back, but this wasn't going to be a completely joyful reunion. He was beyond thankful she was alive, that her kidnapper hadn't killed her all those years ago. But it was possible someone didn't want her alive. Maybe the same someone who'd kidnapped her and murdered their parents.

"I'll have to tell her," Theo muttered. "*We'll* tell her," he amended.

Kim made a sound of agreement and held on. There was no fire-hot attraction in this embrace. Just the need to comfort each other, something they hadn't been able to do in over twenty years.

She eased back, her gaze automatically locking with his, and even though the shock was still on her face, Kim also managed a slight smile. "Faith's alive," she said in a whisper.

Yeah, and maybe it was because of that smile he lost his mind for a couple of seconds and brushed his mouth over hers. It was barely a touch, but man, it hit him hard. Just as he'd known it would. There would never be any such thing as casual kisses between them. Not with this heat.

"Sorry," he murmured. But the apology was a lie. He wasn't sorry at all and, in that moment, he knew something else.

That there would be other kisses.

The danger and Faith showing up had snapped something inside him, and he no longer wanted to keep his hands off Kim. He could use those old adages about life being short and never knowing what tomorrow would hold because they definitely applied here. Maybe she felt the same because her eyes stayed locked with his a few seconds more before she finally muttered some profanity and stepped back.

"The hospital," she said. "I'm guessing you have enough deputies there, so we won't be going with backup."

He nodded and wasn't even sure he had backup available here. Still, he'd take precautions, and they'd make the short trip in a cruiser just in case the shooter decided to fire any more bullets at them. First though, he had a call to make.

Theo pressed the number for Deputy Norris who would still be at Nadia's with Jack and the nanny. He had to make sure his son was okay.

"Everything's fine here," the deputy immediately said.

Some relief cut through the tension in his chest. "Good. Has Nadia made it back yet?" Theo had arranged for a reserve deputy to escort her home from the hospital, but he hadn't heard back on that.

"She just called and should be here within the hour," Norris verified. In the background, Theo heard his son's chatter. "I think Jack wants to say hello to you."

Despite everything else going on, Theo smiled when Jack came on the line. "Daddy, you see me soon?"

Not soon enough, and Theo silently cursed that. His time with his son was precious, and he hated that he couldn't be there.

"Sorry, but I won't be able to pick you up this morning," he told Jack. Hopefully soon though. "Daddy loves you, and I'll be over to see you as soon as I can."

"Love you, too. Bye-bye," Jack tacked onto that, and he must have handed the phone back to Norris because the deputy spoke a moment later.

"Don't worry," Norris said. "I'll keep him safe."

"Thanks." And Theo meant that, too. It was a huge relief to know his little boy was being protected. "One more thing. Make sure Quill and Rowena don't come near Jack. As of now, they're both suspects in the attack at the hospital."

"Will do," Norris assured him.

Once Theo put his phone away, Kim and he grabbed their coats and when Theo opened his office door, he saw a welcome sight. Mason Ryland was standing there waiting, as if reporting for duty. Even though Mason was in his late fifties now, Theo knew he was capable of still kicking some butt.

And he sported a scowl that proved it.

Deputy Nelline Rucker was at her desk and was still in the process of taking Rowena's statement, but she looked up at Theo and gave him nonverbal confirmation that Greg had been making a nuisance of himself.

Mason hiked his thumb to Greg, who was sporting a scowl as well. "This guy seems to think the sun revolves around him and that no one has anything more important to do than to cater to his whims. Any chance I can arrest him for something?"

Theo didn't smile, but he appreciated how Mason had a way of spelling out a situation. "No arrest…yet," he added, knowing it would earn him narrowed eyes from Greg. It did.

"I'm standing around here when I need to be talking to my fiancée," Greg groused.

"He keeps saying that," Mason supplied. "Again, it's that 'sun revolving around him' attitude. Hush," he warned Greg when the man opened his mouth again.

Maybe because it sounded like the threat that it was, Greg hushed.

"My client has submitted to the GSR test," Duran volunteered, "but Deputy Rucker said we had to wait for you. Then, this reserve deputy showed up—"

"And I told them they had to wait for you," Mason interrupted.

"They do," Theo attested. He tipped his head to Greg. "He needs to be interviewed as to his whereabouts at the time of the hospital shooting."

Greg huffed, opened his mouth again, but one sharp glance from Mason had him hushing.

"I can interview him," Mason offered. "After that, what should I do with him?"

"If he confesses to any wrongdoing, arrest him. In the meantime, Kim and I have an errand to run."

Mason shifted his attention to Kim and gave her a once-over. "Your mom's worried about you. Should she be?"

"No," Kim said, though that wasn't anywhere near the truth. "I'll call her again after…later," she amended.

Mason's gaze stayed on her a moment before he turned back to Theo. "Call me…later. After you've run this *errand*." He had to know it was an important one for Theo to take Kim out and about. "You've got backup?"

Theo shook his head. "All my deputies are tied up."

"I've finished with Rowena, so I can go with you," Nelline said, standing. "If Mason will hold down the fort here."

"Consider it done," Mason agreed. "Don't get shot," he added to Theo and Kim.

"I expect to be able to see Ashley very soon," Greg snarled to them as they headed out with Nelline.

Theo ignored him, knowing that Mason would be able to keep the man in line. And at the sheriff's office. No way did Theo want Greg showing up at the hospital while he was trying to break the news to Ashley that she was indeed his sister.

The cruiser was parked right out front so, thankfully, they didn't have to be out in the open for more than a couple of seconds while they jumped in. Theo got behind the wheel with Nelline riding shotgun and Kim in the backseat. He'd just pulled away from the station when Kim's phone dinged with a text.

"It's from Hudson," Kim relayed.

Theo knew she meant Hudson Granger, who owned the company that installed and maintained the security equipment on the Silver Creek Ranch. No small endeavor, either, since there were more than a dozen residences there along with the many outbuildings necessary for such a large ranch. Added to that, Hudson also employed private investigators that Kim sometimes used for her cases. Theo knew the man was darn good at his job and trusted him.

"I asked Hudson to take a look at Greg, Duran and the Neelys," Kim relayed. "He's going to try to find out if any of them did any big payoffs or got any big deposits around the time Faith was taken."

Good. Of course, Theo had set up those automated searches to do the same, but it wouldn't hurt to have Hudson looking as well.

"Hudson also requested the report on the car accident that killed the Neelys," Kim added. She met Theo's brief glance in the rearview mirror. "Just in case it wasn't an accident."

Yeah, Theo had already gone there, and it had occurred to him that the person who'd given Faith to the Neelys might have wanted them eliminated since there was no statute of limitations on murder. Of course, that left Theo with a big question. Why had the person waited all those years to tie off that particular loose end? That might be something Ashley could answer.

Or rather, Faith.

He did the mental correction and then silently repeated her name several more times, hoping he could quickly come to terms with her being alive. That's because Faith would no doubt need plenty of help to deal with it. Perhaps plenty of protection, too, if it turned out that someone did want her dead.

However, there was another player when it came to motives for the shooting. Quill. The man hated Kim and

Theo enough to kill, and that meant Theo had to make interviewing Quill a top priority. Then again, he had a lot of priorities at the moment and first he had to find Quill and have him brought in.

There were still plenty of signs of activity when Theo pulled into the hospital parking lot. Along with two cruisers, there were vans for both CSI and the bomb squad. The wind slapped at the yellow crime scene tape that had cordoned off most of the area. Probably so the CSIs and deputies could search for those spent casings or anything else the shooter might have left behind.

"Want me to go in with you?" Nelline asked Theo when he stopped as close as he could to the entrance.

He shook his head. "Go back to the station and make sure Greg isn't giving Mason any trouble."

The deputy chuckled because she almost certainly knew that no one gave Mason trouble for long. Still, there were a ton of reports that needed to be done, and Mason's forte wasn't paperwork. Nelline was best suited for that.

"Just try to track down Quill," Theo added to the deputy as Kim and he got out of the cruiser. "And I'll text you when we need a ride back."

They hurried into the hospital, where there was more activity going on. Theo spotted a bomb squad member packing up equipment. A CSI was examining one of the stairwells, and Grayson was talking to a doctor. His stand-in dad, or "bonus dad" as Theo had always called him, ended his conversation and made a beeline toward him.

"Are you both okay?" Grayson immediately asked.

Kim and he nodded in unison. "We weren't injured," she added.

Grayson made a sound of disagreement. "Maybe not physically. Your mom's worried," he told her, causing Kim to sigh.

"So Uncle Mason said," she verified. "I'll call her as soon as I can. Noah, too." Yeah, she'd need to dole out some reassurances to her brother, who must have been on shift at SAPD or he would have been there.

"You're here to check on things or see the woman you brought in?" Grayson asked, aiming that question at Theo.

"Both. But more the second than the first. I figure you've got things under control here. Thanks for that, by the way."

Grayson waved it off while continuing to study Theo. "You found out something about the woman?" He stopped, groaned. "You have proof that she's Faith?"

"Yeah. Fingerprints," Theo answered.

Grayson dragged in a long breath. "She's in room 112, with Gage guarding her door."

Gage, Kim's uncle and Grayson's brother. He was a retired federal agent and wouldn't let anyone get past him to try to hurt Faith.

"You want me to go with you to tell her?" Grayson asked.

Theo shook his head. "Just keep an eye on things here."

His bonus dad could handle the multifaceted operations of a crime scene of this size. So could Theo. Because Grayson had been the one who'd taught him how to handle such things. But right now, Theo knew he had to focus on Faith.

Kim and he made their way through the hospital, which wasn't huge by anyone's standards, so it only took them a couple of seconds to make it to the hall where the first floor rooms were located. He spotted Gage, who was leaning against the door. He was also wearing a shoulder holster and his reserve deputy's badge.

Gage smiled when he saw them. A real-deal smile despite the nightmare of the past couple of hours, and he brushed a kiss on Kim's cheek.

"How many people have told you that your mom's worried about you?" Gage asked.

"Enough," she answered, and she took out her phone and fired off a text. To her mom, no doubt.

"Were you the shooter's target?" Gage asked and then tipped his head to the door. "Or was she?"

"To be determined," Theo answered. "She's Faith. That's what I'm here to tell her."

Gage's usual cocky expression faded. "Hell."

That about summed up Theo's feelings. A mixture of dread, worry, relief and elation. He tried to tamp all of that down, though, and Kim and he stepped inside.

Faith was in the hospital bed, but she wasn't sleeping. Just the opposite. She was practically sitting at attention, and she had the plastic water pitcher gripped in her hand as if she might plan to use it to defend herself if that became necessary.

"Did you catch the person who tried to kill us?" she immediately asked.

Theo shook his head. "No, I'm sorry."

She lowered the pitcher and sank back against the

pillows. "I've been thinking about the shooting, and I must have been the one the gunman was after."

Even though Theo had to tell her about her real identity, the comment got his attention. "Why do you say that?"

She sighed. "Because the gunman could have gotten to you other times. I mean, you both live here in Silver Creek. But no one shot at you until I was with you."

That was a good theory, but Theo immediately saw the flaw in it. "It could be the timing just worked out better for the shooter. Or maybe he wanted us to believe you were the target."

Her eyes widened. "Why would he want you to believe that?"

"To throw suspicion off himself and onto someone else," Kim readily provided. She glanced at Theo. "Because of our jobs, both Theo and I have made enemies. The shooter might be one of them."

Faith seemed to consider that a moment and then she nodded. Paused. "Could it have been Greg?"

Again, that stopped Theo from spilling the news they'd come to tell her. "Why would you think that?"

She lifted her shoulder. "I think he knows I'm having second thoughts about marrying him, and he could be angry." But then she shook her head. "He's never been violent with me, though, so he probably wouldn't try to hurt me."

"You're having second thoughts about continuing the engagement?" Kim prompted, taking the question right out of Theo's mouth.

Faith didn't exactly jump into an explanation. She

took a couple of moments. "My parents wanted me to marry him. Or rather, they pressed me to marry him," she amended. "But now that they're no longer alive, I don't feel that pressure, and it's making me want to call off the engagement."

"You were planning on marrying Greg because you wanted to please your parents?" Theo asked.

Faith winced a little. "I know how that sounds, but the therapist at the hospital talked to me about this. It sometimes happens with adopted kids. The child is so grateful for the loving family that she wants to please the adoptive parents." She drew in a long breath. "But I'm seeing there's a fine line between pleasing and bending to their will."

And Greg was part of that bending. It explained how Faith could end up with a man like that, but Theo had to wonder—why had the Neelys wanted their adoptive daughter, a daughter they seemingly loved, to be with a domineering man with a temper?

Unfortunately, a reason quickly came to mind.

If Greg had been the one to kidnap Faith and commit two murders, then he might have blackmailed or "pressured" the Neelys by reminding them they could end up in jail right along with him. Of course, that would mean the Neelys had known what'd happened. Maybe their knowledge hadn't come until after the crimes had already been committed, but they still could have been charged as accessories after the fact.

Theo's phone dinged with a text and he glanced at the screen to see that the CSI has already run the GSR test on Greg.

Negative.

That didn't mean the man hadn't been the shooter, but Duran could use the results to try to pressure Theo into letting Greg see Faith. But Theo had no intentions of letting that happen.

"Is something wrong?" Faith asked, obviously noticing his reaction to the text.

He put his phone away and met her gaze. "Your fingerprints came back as a match to Faith's." Theo didn't add anything else. He just gave her some time to let that sink in.

Faith gasped, and she tried to speak, but it took her a while to get out the words. "You're sure?"

Theo settled for a nod since he thought he might have trouble getting out words as well. Even though he'd known the truth for about a half hour now, the emotions were still coursing through him.

This was his sister.

Obviously, she'd changed a lot from the eight-year-old kid she'd once been, but now that he had studied her face, he could see Faith.

"It's true," Faith muttered, and she reached out her hand to Kim. Maybe because she was closer than Theo.

"It's true," Kim confirmed, and she not only took Faith's hand, she pulled her into a hug.

That brought about tears of a happy reunion, one that only added to the storm of emotions. Theo was happy, too. Damn happy. But there was another side to this. It was possible someone was trying to kill the sister he'd just found.

Faith motioned for him to come closer, and when

he did, she hooked her other arm around him, pulling him into the hug with Kim and her. Some of the tension that Theo had been carrying for years fell off him. A hefty amount of guilt replaced it. Because he should have found Faith before now. Better yet, he should have stopped her from being kidnapped.

The hug lasted a while, and Theo didn't do anything to put an end to it. Finally, though, Faith eased back and, smiling, she swiped tears from her cheeks.

"Thank you," she said to both Kim and him.

He had no idea why she was thanking them, and he would have let her know that had she not continued before he could say anything.

"But I've brought danger right to your doorstep," Faith added. Her smile vanished and the worry bunched up her forehead.

"You don't know that," Kim assured her. "In fact, Theo and I could be the ones bringing danger to you. Just know that Theo is a darn good cop, and he'll do everything in his power to protect you. So will I."

That caused a fresh round of crying, and Faith turned those tear-filled eyes toward Theo. "I honestly don't have any clear memories of the night I was taken. Just those bits that I've already told you about." Her bottom lip quivered. "You should know that I also had a breakdown after my parents…after the Neelys died. I'm not delusional," she quickly added. "But I did have a breakdown."

Not surprised by that, Theo nodded. "That's why you got help at the hospital in San Antonio?"

"Yes, and I also wanted to try to make sense of those memory fragments I was having."

"Did you ever tell Greg or anyone else about those fragments?" Theo asked.

Faith stared at him and he saw the alarm go through her eyes. "I told Greg. And my parents...the Neelys," she amended. And, judging from the way she shivered, that reminded her that their parents had been murdered.

Maybe killed by the same person who now wanted her dead.

Because a dead person wouldn't have a memory to regain. Especially a memory that could get someone convicted of a double murder and kidnapping.

"I didn't exactly keep the memories a secret," Faith admitted, shivering again. "I should have."

"No," Kim quickly disagreed. "You had no reason to distrust those people." She paused a heartbeat. "Did you?"

Faith wasn't so fast to answer, and that put a knot in his gut. Hell. What had she been through all these years?

"I trusted the Neelys," Faith finally said. "I mean, I always sensed they were keeping something from me, but trust me, I had no idea they were holding back on telling me who I really was. And they might not have known. I can't believe they would have had any part in killing our parents and kidnapping me."

No, but again, there was that after-the-fact possibility. Or maybe the Neelys had learned about it more recently than the night someone would have brought a kidnapped child to them.

"Are you sure the Neelys' car accident was actually an accident?" Theo asked. Bringing this up was a risk because Faith already seemed right on the edge of not being able to hold it together. She was emotionally fragile. Still, the more they knew, the faster they could catch whoever was responsible for the attack.

Faith stared at him a long time. "You think the person who took me killed them to keep them quiet."

"It's a theory," Theo admitted, and he was pleased that instead of another shudder or shiver, he thought she was steeling herself up and trying to grasp the big picture. "That means I have to look at Duran and Greg as persons of interest."

She nodded. "*Persons of interest*. That's a cop's way of saying suspects."

In this case, yes. They were indeed suspects.

"What I need you to do is write down the names of anyone close to the Neelys, anyone who might have had a part in what happened," Theo instructed. "Think back to anything that was said about when they adopted you. *Anything*," he emphasized.

Theo could see that was the right thing to do. It gave her a task, something that could help the investigation. There was also something else she might be able to help them with.

"By any chance, have you sent Kim letters over the past fourteen years?" he asked.

Faith immediately shook her head. "No, I haven't. I didn't know until recently who Kim was. What kinds of letters?"

"Ones connected to that night your folks were killed

since they're addressed to Kimmie, the nickname everyone called me back then," Kim provided. "All of them say *Help me. Please help me.*"

Faith looked at Theo. "That's what I called out that night?"

He settled for a nod since his throat and chest had tightened again, and Kim filled in the rest for him. "But those weren't your exact words. It's more of a generic version of what you said."

Faith nodded slowly. "So, maybe the killer isn't the one sending the letters to you."

Kim made a sound of agreement. "The letters could be horrible pranks."

Theo was still holding on to that hope. As bad as pranks like that would be—and they were bad—it would be worse if the killer was sending them as some kind of unfinished business.

"I don't know of anyone who'd send letters like that," Faith insisted. "But I will make a list of the Neelys' friends and acquaintances. Their employees, too." She paused. "How long will I have to be here?"

"Unfortunately, you'll have to stay a while longer," Theo told her "but I'll arrange to have a laptop brought in for you. Pen and paper, too, if that's how you'd rather create that list."

Faith nodded, swallowed hard. "What if the killer comes after me here?"

"He won't get in," he quickly assured her. "Right now, Gage Ryland is on the door, and no one will get past him."

Theo could see the wariness in her eyes. But there

was trust, too. He was her big brother. The sheriff of Silver Creek. And he was going to do something he hadn't managed when she was eight.

He was going to make sure she was safe.

"I don't want to go with Greg when it's time for me to leave," Faith said. "Can I go with you?" She glanced at both Kim and Theo.

"Yes," Theo assured her. "I don't live at our old house." Too many bad memories. "I have a small ranch."

He was about to explain he could take Faith there. Or to Kim's. But his phone rang, and when he saw Ava's number, he knew he had to take the call.

"I found something," the deputy said the moment Theo answered. "I'm sending it to you now." His phone dinged with an incoming message. "It's some still images taken from the hospital surveillance camera about five minutes before the first shot was fired."

Theo didn't put the call on speaker in case Ava had news that would upset Faith even more than she already was, but he did have a look at the trio of photos.

And Theo cursed when he saw the man's face.

Chapter Eight

Kim hurried to Theo, and she immediately saw what had caused him to curse. She wanted to curse, too.

Because it was Quill in the photos.

No mistaking that, and judging from the timestamp for when he disappeared out of camera range and into the hospital, he would have had time to go up the stairs to the roof and start shooting.

"He's not carrying a rifle," Kim pointed out. But that didn't mean Quill hadn't been the shooter. "He's got a backpack, so it could have been a firearm that he assembled on scene."

In fact, any of their suspects could have done that. Or even planted the weapon there earlier. Faith had been in the hospital for well over a half hour before the bomb scare had happened.

We'll keep checking the surveillance footage, Ava texted.

Good because Kim was certain that Theo would want to know when Quill had exited the building. Greg or Duran as well. It was possible, though, that none of them had been the gunman, that they could have hired someone to do the job.

"I need to have Quill tested for GSR," Theo muttered, and after he put away his phone, he looked at Faith. "I'll arrange for that laptop so you can get started on those names."

Faith gave a shaky nod. Shaky because their reaction to the text had no doubt alarmed her. "This man, Quill, could have been the one who tried to kill me?" she asked.

"If Quill was the shooter, then he was gunning for Kim or me, not you," Theo corrected. "Kim is the prosecuting attorney at his upcoming trial, and I was the arresting officer."

Faith's face stayed tight. "Please, both of you be careful. I don't want to lose either of you."

"We'll be careful," Kim assured her.

That wasn't just lip service either. They would both be on high alert, and that meant doing something that would break down more of those long erected barriers.

They'd have to stay together.

Yes, she could get protection from another Silver Creek lawman. Heaven knew she had enough of those in her family. But she wanted Theo safe, too, and that meant being together so they could watch each other's backs.

They said their goodbyes to Faith, both Theo and Kim hugging the woman. It wasn't exactly like old times, but Kim didn't have any doubts now that this was her childhood friend. No doubts, either, that Theo and Faith could start to rebuild their relationship once the threat of the danger had passed.

When they went out of the room and back into the hall, Theo texted Nelline so she could return to the hospital with the cruiser. Theo added a Be careful as they made their way to the exit. It wouldn't take the deputy long to get there, and Kim knew they wouldn't be going back outside until the cruiser was in sight.

"Are we going to Quill's house?" Kim asked.

"No." Theo didn't even hesitate. "I want Quill to cooperate with a GSR test, and he won't do that if you and I show up. It'd be like waving a red flag in front of a pissed-off bull."

It would indeed. Theo would have no trouble getting a warrant for a GSR test, but it would go even faster if a pair of deputies could get the man to do it voluntarily. And Quill just might do that if he thought it would prevent him from being arrested—something that would happen if he refused the test.

"Agreed," she said. "But if the CSIs clear it, I would like to drop by my house and get some things." She paused a heartbeat until his gaze met hers. "I figured it'd be better to stay at your place."

She knew the suggestion wouldn't come as a surprise to him. His ranch would be easier to secure than her house because he had hands who could keep watch. Added to that, she knew he had a topnotch security system since she'd heard her own security specialist, Hudson, mention that he'd personally done the work at Theo's.

"Or we could go to the Silver Creek Ranch and stay

with either my folks or Uncle Grayson and Aunt Eve," she added.

Kim could practically see him working his way through those options. "My place," he finally said. "When Faith gets out of the hospital either later today or tomorrow, it might be overwhelming for her to stay at the Silver Creek Ranch."

No way could Kim argue with him about that. The ranch was indeed overwhelming and was larger than some small towns. Yes, it was secure, but she thought they could make Theo's equally safe while not adding more stress for Faith. Of course, the ultimate stress reliever for all of them would be to catch the person who'd fired those shots and stop him from launching another attack.

"It's nearly lunchtime," Theo noted a few seconds later. "You need to eat," he insisted when she was about to say she wasn't hungry. "After we get your things from your house, we can go back to my office, order some food and dig into the investigation. I need to go over the statements from Rowena, Greg and Duran."

Yes, because any of the three might have said something that would give them clues about the shooter. She could also go tit for tat here and make sure he ate something as well.

"I also want Quill found, tested for GSR and then brought in for questioning," Theo spelled out while he sent a text to Ava, telling her to make that happen.

Maybe Ava wouldn't have any trouble finding the man. Or bringing Quill in. But no way would Ava go to Quill's alone. She'd take backup, and if the man resisted, then the deputies would have solid grounds to arrest him.

When Nelline pulled the cruiser to a stop directly outside the ER doors, Theo flipped off the safety strap on his holster so his weapon would be ready, and he hurried them out of there. Theo sat in front with Nelline and Kim took the back.

As she drove away, and while everyone kept watch around them, the deputy began giving Theo updates on the various reports she'd been getting from the CSIs and the lab. Kim very much wanted to hear what Nelline was saying, but her phone rang. When she saw the name on the screen, she knew it was a call she had to take.

"It's Hudson," Kim relayed to Theo just as she answered it.

"I've found out a few things," Hudson immediately said to her. "Ashley didn't lie when she said she'd voluntarily committed herself to the hospital. No one can force her to go back." He paused a moment. "FYI, don't ask me how I learned this, but Ashley actually is Faith Sheldon."

It shouldn't have surprised her that he'd managed to confirm that because Hudson was the best at tracking down info. "Yes, Theo just told her about her prints being a match to his sister. Faith has finally come home," she added in a murmur.

She glanced up, meeting Theo's gaze, and she saw both the relief and the worry in his eyes. This would no doubt trigger a new round of grief for him. No way to avoid that since it would also trigger the memories. That meant both of them were in for a hard night. Faith, too.

"You want me to keep digging on Faith to see what she's been doing for the past twenty-one years?" Hudson asked.

"Yes," she answered. Even though they were going behind the woman's back, it was best for Theo and Kim to have as many pieces of this puzzle as possible. One of those pieces might lead them to the shooter.

"Will do. I also got some more on Greg and Duran," Hudson went on, and Kim went ahead and put the call on speaker since it appeared Nelline was done with her updates. "Greg's made some lousy investments over the years, and I've found two occasions where the Neelys bailed him out."

"Why?" Kim had to ask. "I mean how is it they were so close to Greg?"

"You want to know if they were paying him off to keep him quiet about who their daughter really was."

"Yes," Kim verified.

"No actual proof of that *yet*," Hudson admitted, emphasizing that last word to let her know he was still looking in that area. "I'm sure Greg would say the Neelys gave him the money because of their longtime friendship with him and his late parents. But it's a lot of money. Nearly a quarter of a million, if you tally up both times they did the bailout."

It certainly felt like hush money to her, especially since Greg didn't seem to have a winning personality to instill that closeness to the Neelys. But maybe the couple thought of Greg as the son they'd never had rather than a kidnapper and killer who'd provided them with a daughter.

"You said you found something on Duran?" she prompted as Nelline took the turn into the driveway of Kim's house. Kim glanced around but didn't see anyone, including any of the CSI team.

"Oh, yeah," Hudson declared. "Definitely not squeaky clean. He's been investigated for embezzlement and money laundering. Nothing seems to stick, though, since he's never been charged with anything. But are you ready for this? There's a rumor that Duran has brokered some black market adoptions."

Theo's head whipped up. That obviously got his attention. "This is Theo," he spoke up. "Any facts to back up those rumors?"

"Working on it," Hudson assured him. "But my researchers dug up some old social media posts where two people in Kerrville were gushing thanks to Duran for finding them a baby and arranging a private adoption. I can send you the couple's names or talk to them myself."

Theo stayed quiet a moment. "Send me the names but keep digging to see what you can find on them. And on Duran."

"Will do," Hudson assured him. "I'll get back to you as soon as I have anything."

They ended the call just as Nelline pulled to a stop in front of Kim's house. "Wait here," Theo instructed the deputy. "And make some calls. I want the adoption paperwork the Neelys filled out. My guess is Duran handled that."

Yes, and that could possibly include him finding the child for them. Even if the paperwork did lead back to Duran, though, he could always claim he had no idea that Ashley was actually Faith. No way would he admit to anything connected to the kidnapping since there'd been two murders involved.

"The CSIs are done with their search," Nelline explained when Kim glanced around the yard. "They said they locked up."

That was good because the locks would have automatically engaged the security system. Kim used the app on her phone to disengage her security system and unlock the door so that Theo and she could hurry into her house.

Even though it'd only been hours since they were last here, it felt much longer. Probably because so much had happened. This had been one of those "lives changing on a dime" mornings.

She glanced around and didn't see anything out of place, but that didn't mean the deputies and the CSIs hadn't done a thorough search. They'd just taken more care than usual because of her family's connections to law enforcement.

"According to the update I got," Theo said, doing his own glancing around, "there were no signs that the man we saw actually got inside the house."

That was good, but it had to be ruled out. "How about the barn? Did they find anything in there?"

Theo shook his head and followed her as she made her way to her bedroom to pack a few things. He didn't go in with her but instead stopped in the doorway and bracketed his hands on the frame. Then again, he didn't have to be closer for her to feel him, and she knew he was watching her. Maybe just looking for signs that the hellish morning was going to make her break. Maybe because they just had trouble keeping their eyes off each other.

That was certainly the case with her.

"What else did Nelline fill you in on?" she asked, taking her small suitcase from the closet. Best to try to stay focused on the investigation.

"It was more of filling me in on what we don't have. They found shell casings but got no prints off them. Ava and Jesse are going out to Quill's to deal with him. Your uncle Kade is doing reserve deputy duty by going through the rest of the feed from the surveillance camera at the hospital."

Kim had to hope that some or all of that would give them the answers they needed because the sooner the shooter was caught, the sooner her life could get back to normal.

But she rethought that—after she made the mistake of glancing at Theo again.

He certainly made a picture standing there in the doorway. He'd kept on his coat, but it was open, revealing his shirt. And the muscles beneath it. She'd had an up-close-and-personal encounter with those muscles earlier when they'd hugged.

Theo made a sound, a sort of throat clearing, and that's when Kim realized her hands had frozen and she was blatantly just staring at him. Theo was staring back, and the heat was zinging between them.

Kim made her own sound, a weary sigh, and after zipping the suitcase, she picked it up and went to him.

"This is a mistake," she said. "But I'm having a hard time remembering why it's a mistake."

The corner of his mouth lifted in that sizzling smile that could be considered foreplay to a really hot round of sex. The timing was all wrong for her to be having a reaction like that to him. All wrong and yet somehow right. Of course, that "right" feeling was because of the urging of certain parts of her body, but Kim went with it anyway.

She leaned in and brushed her mouth over his.

Talk about a hard slam of lust. Pure, hot lust. There was no other word for it. No words, either, for the avalanche of feelings she got when Theo let go of the doorjamb to slide his hand around the back of her neck and pull her to him. He put his mouth to hers, and it wasn't a brush. It was a full-pressure, scalding kiss she felt in every inch of her.

Oh, mercy.

He was good at this. Of course, he was. This was Theo, the man she'd fantasized about for years, so it would have been next to impossible for him to let her down with that clever mouth of his.

Kim made a sound of pleasure and heard Theo make a version of the same. There was no hesitancy in those sounds. No hesitancy in the kiss either. He went for long and deep. For a kiss that was begging her to latch onto him and do something about this fire and need he'd been building in her for years.

But she forced herself to stop and ease back.

Emphasis on "forced" because there was no way her body wanted her to quit. Theo was no doubt going through the same experience, and she had proof of that with the next sound he made. Not pleasure but frustration.

He muttered a choice curse word, his warm breath hitting against her mouth and instantly making her regret she'd been the one to put an end to it. She didn't have time to deal with that regret for long, though, because Theo's phone rang, and she saw Nelline's name on the screen.

She watched as Theo took a couple of seconds to shake off the effects of that mind-numbing kiss and fortify himself before he answered. "Is everything okay?" he asked.

"Maybe," the deputy answered. "A truck just turned into Kim's driveway, and I'm pretty sure it's Quill Odell."

Chapter Nine

Theo definitely wanted to interrogate Quill, but he darn sure didn't want it to happening here at Kim's. She'd already been through enough today without coming face-to-face with the man who was a prime suspect in the shooting that could have killed her.

He went to the window at the front of the house and confirmed that it was indeed Quill. The man parked his truck next to the cruiser and got out. At least it didn't appear that Quill was ready to go on the run. There also weren't any weapons in his hands. That didn't mean, though, that he wasn't carrying. Nelline would have known that, and that's why she'd gotten out of the cruiser and was in the process of frisking him.

Quill was a big man. Six-three with plenty of muscle even though he was now in his fifties. He wore a black stocking cap, but Theo knew that beneath it Quill had shaved his balding head.

Kim joined Theo at the window, and she glanced at him. "It appears Quill has something he wants to say," she remarked when Quill started cursing the deputy for patting him down.

"Yeah." Theo sighed. "Any chance you'll stay put and let me handle this?"

She looked him straight in the eyes and he saw she wasn't happy with that idea. "Since he's at my house, it's likely he's come to talk to me. You could be the 'red flag to the bull' scenario, and since you'll want to question him, then it'll be best if he finishes whatever business he feels he has with me."

He couldn't dispute that. Theo knew he always seemed to bring out the worst in Quill. Probably because Quill was well aware that Theo despised him.

"I'll have Quill come onto the porch, and we can both stand inside while you talk to him." Theo spelled it out for her. "Nelline can get back in the cruiser just in case Quill is innocent in the hospital shooting and the actual gunman is still out there. And if Quill tries to start any trouble, you'll get out of the doorway."

Kim nodded. "I'll get out of the way, but I do have my gun just in case things get ugly." She pointed to the back waist of her jeans where there was no doubt a slide holster.

As compromises went, it was a good one, but he still would have preferred her not having to put herself through this. It was never easy to deal with Quill, and he was bound to be in an especially bad mood since he'd likely heard he was a suspect in the shooting.

Theo opened the door about halfway, and he kept his hand on his gun. "Let him come to the porch," he called out to the deputy. "You get back in the cruiser."

The deputy immediately did as he said, but she lowered the window, no doubt so she could still provide him with some backup. But he had backup right next to him since Kim knew how to handle a firearm.

As Quill began approaching the porch steps, Theo recited the Miranda warning to him. Of course, that riled the man, but Theo didn't want anything Quill might say to be inadmissible because he hadn't been read his rights.

"All that's not necessary," Quill growled, his gaze and index finger going straight to Kim. "I hear you're trying to get my bail revoked."

"You're a person of interest in a shooting," Kim admitted. "Revocation of bail comes with the territory."

First, though, Theo and Kim would have to convince a judge that Quill was guilty. Right now they had circumstantial evidence with the surveillance footage, but that alone wouldn't be enough for revocation of bail. That's why neither Kim nor Theo had started the process. Apparently, though, Quill believed they had.

Quill cursed. "I had nothing to do with that shooting. Nothing." He spat the word out. "Somebody's trying to set me up."

"But you were at the hospital at the time of the incident," Theo quickly pointed out.

Quill's eyes widened a moment, only a moment, before he covered his surprise about Theo having known that. "I was," he admitted. "Because I heard about you bringing in the woman you found, and I wanted to see what was going on."

Either that was a really bad "wrong time, wrong place" deal, or Quill was lying. "Then, if you're innocent, you'll submit to a test to detect gunshot residue," Theo countered.

The man shook his head, muttered more profanity. "And if I don't, I guess you'll toss me in jail."

Theo nodded. "I will."

He expected that to bring on a round of vicious profanity, but Quill merely shook his head and gave a resigned sigh. "All right. When and where do I get the test?"

Theo took out his phone and requested a deputy to come to Kim's to collect the man. "About ten minutes at the sheriff's office," Theo informed him. "And then you'll be questioned about what you were doing at the hospital because I've never thought of you as a curious man. Seems far-fetched that you'd just want to be up on the latest gossip."

He sighed again. "A friend texted me and said this woman might be your long-lost sister. I knew your mom and dad, even did a little work for them on their ranch, and I knew both you and your sister. I just wanted to know if it was Faith, especially since you were once married to my daughter and are my grandson's father."

Quill had indeed done some work for his folks, and it didn't surprise him that there'd been talk about the woman being his sister. The EMTs or someone on the medical staff could have known the mystery woman's prints were being taken. But what was puzzling was why that would interest Quill.

And that puzzlement gave Theo a really bad feeling in his gut.

Because, what if Quill had had something to do with

Faith being kidnapped? If so, he would want to make sure she didn't incriminate him in any way.

Theo glanced at Kim to see if she was following along on this mental thread. He was pretty sure she was.

"I didn't go to the hospital to shoot anyone," Quill insisted. The silent response Theo and Kim were giving the man seemed to make him uncomfortable. Or maybe Quill just knew they were piecing together a very bad possibility.

That they were looking into the face of the man who'd murdered his parents.

"So, you were curious enough to drive to the hospital," Theo summarized, "and be in the same area where shots were fired. FYI, before you answer, know that surveillance footage from the security camera is being analyzed as we speak."

Quill opened his mouth and then seemed to rethink what he'd been about to say. "Rowena knew I was at the hospital. She drove past the parking lot as I was getting out of my truck."

Theo gave the man a flat look. "Are you saying Rowena fired those shots to set you up?"

Quill gave a firm nod. "That's exactly what I'm saying. If she didn't pull the trigger herself, she could have got somebody else to do it. I think Rowena would do anything to make sure I'm put away for good."

"Really?" Kim said, the sarcasm heavy in her voice. "The woman you battered for years would do this?"

But Quill ignored Kim's tone. "Yeah. She would. Rowena's got a mean streak, and she's playing all nice with the likes of you, but I think she's got it in for me."

The woman deserved to have it in for Quill after what he'd done to her, but Theo kept that to himself. Before the deputy arrived to take Quill in, Theo wanted more info from the man, and pointing out the obvious wasn't the way to go about getting those answers.

"I know you were questioned about my parents' murders, but thinking back, do you recall anything suspicious going on in the days or even weeks leading up to their deaths?"

Theo tried to keep anything accusatory out of the question, and it must have worked because he didn't see any of the usual anger flare up in Quill's eyes.

"No." Quill said that on a sigh. "I've gone over all of that plenty of times, and like I told Grayson way back then, I didn't see anybody who could have done that."

Theo had known that was a long shot, but he'd had to try. Sometimes, people did recall little things years after the fact, and on rare occasions, those little things provided clues to help solve the case.

"Is that woman your sister?" Quill asked. "Because she's the one who'd be the best person to give you answers about your folks' murders."

Theo took a moment to decide how he wanted to answer. It wouldn't take long for word to get out that Ashley was Faith. No way to keep that a secret. So, he'd use the info and gauge Quill's reaction to it.

"She's Faith," Theo confirmed.

Quill's face registered surprise before he quickly shut it down and tried to make his expression blank. "So, she knows who took her and did those murders."

"No." Theo needed to make this very clear so that

Faith wouldn't be a target. "She doesn't have any memories of that night."

Not the truth. She did have those fragments, and with some help, she might recall more. And that was the reason she would stay in protective custody until the danger had passed.

Quill shook his head. "I guess that's expected," he murmured. "Poor kid, she had to be traumatized by what she saw and what happened to her."

Yeah, Theo had been, too, and he had to wonder if Quill was the person responsible for that nightmare. Because of Quill's association with Theo's parents, the man had been a person of interest. Quill had been questioned, and questioned hard, but he'd never admitted to any wrongdoing. Nor had there ever been any evidence uncovered to point the finger at him.

However, Theo needed to take another look at the interview notes to see if he could spot any inconsistencies.

"I'm glad you got your sister back and all," Quill went on a moment later, "but what are you going to do about Rowena trying to set me up?" He slid glances at both Theo and Kim.

"Give me the names of someone Rowena could have talked into firing those shots to set you up," Theo simply said. "And I'll investigate."

"I don't know the names of people she considers her friends," Quill insisted. "Heck, she might not have even known the person. You can hire gunmen off the internet."

Yes, you could, but Theo couldn't see Rowena having ready knowledge of how to do that. Still, he'd check.

"Think of names," Theo instructed as he saw the cruiser turn into the driveway. Jesse was behind the wheel. "Also, did you leave a dead animal on Rowena's doorstep?" he tagged on.

Oh, that caused the ugly anger to rise again. "Hell, no. Did Rowena say I'd done that? Because if she did, she's lying through her teeth."

Theo had no intentions of informing Quill of what Rowena had said, but he needed to give the man a reminder to keep him away from his wife. "If you go near Rowena, you'll be arrested, and your bail will be revoked."

That didn't tamp down any of Quill's temper. However, he didn't spew out any threats.

Jesse pulled the cruiser to a stop and Theo held up his finger in a wait-a-second gesture so he could ask Quill one last question. "Do you know anything about letters that someone's been sending Kim?"

Judging from the stare Quill gave him, he hadn't been expecting the question. But the man didn't immediately dismiss it, either, or snarl out a denial that he'd had any part in doing that.

"Letters," Quill muttered. And it wasn't a question. Traces of the anger vanished and some smugness crept into his expression. "Yeah, I might know something about that. I think Rowena's the one who's been sending those letters to Kim."

Chapter Ten

Kim felt everything inside her go still. Then she remembered who'd just made that accusation.

Quill. A man who couldn't be trusted.

Obviously, Theo felt the same way because he huffed. "Why would Rowena want to send letters to Kim?" He didn't add especially letters that clearly meant to taunt her with the events of that horrible night.

"I told you Rowena likes to make people think she's nice and all, but she's got a mean streak," Quill insisted. "But a couple of years ago, when we were still together, I walked in on her typing something on that old typewriter she kept on the top shelf of her closet."

The letters had indeed been typewritten, but Kim still wasn't convinced. "What made you think she was writing to me? Did you see what she'd typed?"

"I didn't see. She snatched it out of the typewriter and wadded it into a ball, but right before that, she'd been complaining about you." Quill aimed his attention at Kim to let her know he'd meant her. "Like I said, that was when we were still together, still trying to make things work between us, and Rowena wasn't happy that you were pressing her to file charges against me for…a disagreement me and her had."

The "disagreement" was Quill had blackened both of Rowena's eyes and dislocated her shoulder. When Rowena had gone to the hospital, they'd reported the injuries, and Kim had indeed tried to talk the woman into filing charges after Grayson, who was then sheriff, had failed to convince her to do that.

"When did this happen?" Theo demanded. "When did you see Rowena typing the letter?"

Quill's forehead creased. "A few years back. Maybe four or five years ago."

The letters had begun arriving six years ago, around the same time Kim had started working in the district attorney's office, so the timing could fit. *Could*. But there was another possibility.

"You could have used the typewriter as well," Kim pointed out, knowing it would earn her a glare and a denial.

It did. Quill's reaction was fast and filled with instant venom. Oh, yes, he had a quick trigger on that temper.

"I'm trying to help you," Quill snapped, "and you accuse me of something I didn't do."

She shrugged. "It was merely an observation since you admitted you knew the location of the typewriter."

More anger came, and this time his nostrils actually flared, making her think of that bull about to charge the waving red flag. "This conversation is over." He turned and headed down the porch steps.

"Sorry about that," Kim muttered to Theo as they watched Quill storm his way to the waiting cruiser.

"Not to worry. It was good to see his reaction to being accused of writing those letters."

It was, but Kim wished she had a magic lie detector to know if Quill had indeed written them, if Rowena had, or if neither of them had had anything to do with it.

"When will you bring Rowena in for questioning?" Kim asked.

"Soon," Theo assured her. "But first I'll get a warrant to pick up the typewriter from her house. I don't want to alert her to what's going on in case she decides to toss it somewhere."

"Good point. But even if she did write them, it doesn't mean she actually had anything to do with the murders and Faith's kidnapping."

"No," Theo agreed. He didn't shut the door until Quill was in the cruiser with Jesse and they'd driven away. "Finish packing while I get the warrant started," he said, taking out his phone to do that. "Then let's get your things to my place, and we can work from there for a while until we have both the typewriter and Rowena in custody."

Kim got moving, but she felt her anxiety rise some more. Not solely because of the worry of going back outside where they could end up in the path of the shooter but because she was going to Theo's.

A place she'd avoided.

Then again, she could say the same for Theo. But it wasn't possible to avoid him now, not with the danger bearing down on them. Besides, they wouldn't actually be alone for long since Faith would be joining them as soon as she was released from the hospital.

By the time she'd gathered the rest of her things and gone back to the door, Theo had obviously finished his call about the warrant for the typewriter because he was now talking to his head ranch hand, Rusty Chavez. She heard him mention Rusty's name along with giving the hands instructions for the security measures he needed at the ranch.

"We're all set," Theo told her once he'd finished the call. He stopped, took a deep breath. The kind of breath a man took when he was steeling himself up. "I want to swing by Nadia's and check on Jack. I know it's risky—"

"It's something you need to do," she interrupted. She didn't have to be a parent to know how much Theo loved his son. "If you think it'll be awkward for me to be in the cruiser when you do that, I can wait at the sheriff's office or at your place."

Kim saw some of the tension ease from his face, but there was still plenty of worry and concern in his eyes. Worry no doubt because going anywhere could mean making themselves easier targets.

"It'll be awkward no matter what we do," he said, and she knew he was talking about more than just this visit. "But if you're in the cruiser, it'll save time. We can go straight from Nadia's to my place."

She nodded, well aware that he hadn't spelled out that he'd also have to tell Nadia about his houseguest, one who always spurred a mountain of jealousy for his ex. Yep. Theo had needed that steeling-up breath he'd taken.

"You can use your phone to lock up?" he asked as he picked up her suitcase.

"I can." She grabbed her purse and her laptop bag while she pulled up the app to do that. The moment they were on the porch, she secured the house, and they hurried to the cruiser.

"I'll need to go to Nadia's before heading to my place," Theo relayed to Nelline before he made a call to Ava to check for updates.

Nadia's house wasn't far—nothing was "far" in Silver Creek—but Kim decided to spend the five minutes that it would take to get there texting Hudson. She asked for a price quote on a security camera for Rowena's house. It might turn out to be unnecessary if they found out that Rowena had planted the dead rat. Still, there was a good chance that the woman was innocent of any wrongdoing and that Quill had simply wanted to stir up trouble for her with his accusations.

Kim thought back through the letters she'd gotten over the years. If the typewriter that Quill had mentioned actually existed, it could be tested, and a match would point the finger at both Quill and Rowena. However, since the letters had been postmarked from all over Texas, it might be possible to track the couple's whereabouts during those dates.

She got a quick reply from Hudson on the price just as the deputy pulled the cruiser into the driveway at Nadia's. The house was on a quiet street just on the edge of town, and Kim immediately spotted the cruiser. She recalled that Deputy Norris was doing protection detail, but since he wasn't in the cruiser, that hopefully meant he was inside.

"I won't be long," Theo muttered as he got out.

Obviously, Norris had either heard the approaching vehicle or Theo had alerted him to the visit because the deputy opened the door before Theo even reached it. The angle was right for Kim to also see Nadia. She was standing back, holding Jack, and the moment the little boy saw Theo, he shouted out a very happy, "Daddy." Theo went to him, pulling his son into his arms for a long hug.

Kim felt something she didn't want to feel. A longing. She'd always wanted a child, but she hadn't wanted to go the single parent route, and she had never met a man she loved enough to marry.

Well, she had met him, but he had been off limits.

She sighed and admitted to herself that she could have loved Theo enough if the past hadn't always come between them. If they'd both been able to get beyond the grief and loss of that night. However, that grief and loss seemed to be healing now that Faith had returned. That didn't mean they had a clear road ahead though. No. And she got proof of that when she looked at Nadia again.

The woman was staring at her, and while Kim couldn't hear what she was saying to Theo, she figured it was some unpleasant comment because Theo had just informed her that Kim would be his houseguest. Kim didn't want his ex's jealousy playing into her feelings for Theo.

But it did.

Because, in turn, the jealousy could cause more tensions between Nadia and Theo. No way did Kim want that when a precious little boy would be caught in the middle.

Theo handed Jack back to Nadia and, giving Jack a kiss on the cheek, he turned and walked out of the house. Nadia managed to shoot Kim one last glare before the deputy shut the front door.

Kim didn't say anything to Theo when he returned to the cruiser and they started the drive to his ranch. There was nothing to say. She'd apologized so many times for Nadia's feelings toward her, but another "I'm so sorry" wasn't going to fix this. Maybe nothing would.

And that riled her.

Kim didn't care much for that jab of anger, either, but it was there, and she admitted something else to herself. She resented Nadia's totally unwarranted jealousy. Or at least it had been until today. Until today, Theo and she hadn't kissed. They'd kept their hands off each other. But since Kim didn't like lying to herself, she figured there'd be more kissing. And worse, Theo and she would just end up growing closer and closer.

She forced her thoughts off Theo and kept watch out the windows as they drove. Even though this wasn't that far out of town, it was very much in the country. There were woods on each side of the road, and those woods soon turned to pastures as they approached Theo's ranch, Willow Woods—a name he'd taken from the ranch where his mom had been raised.

Nelline took the turn off the road and Theo's house soon came into view. Definitely not small like her own house. This was a two-story Victorian that had once belonged to a family with four kids. Since Theo had bought the place after Nadia and he had divorced, Kim figured he hadn't had more children in mind, not in the near future anyway, but he'd wanted plenty of room for Jack and the horses he boarded, bred, raised and trained.

Kim spotted one of the ranch hands delivering hay to the livestock in the front pasture. The guy was armed, and he immediately looked up, no doubt to make sure it wasn't a gunman trying to get onto the grounds. There was a second hand, also armed, near the front of the house.

"You can drop us off and head back to the office," Theo told the deputy. "See what you can do to hurry the search warrant I've got started for Rowena's house, and if the woman comes into the station before I get back there, call me first so I can give you some interview questions."

"Will do," the deputy assured him and, when she pulled to a stop in front of his house, Theo disengaged the locks and Kim and he hurried up the steps. The moment they were safely inside, he reset the security system.

It wasn't the first time she'd been here. She'd come years ago back in high school because she'd dated a boy who'd lived here, but Kim had avoided the place after Theo bought it.

"Wow," she muttered. "You've redecorated and removed some walls." She stopped, gave a nervous laugh. "Or someone did in the past sixteen years."

"I did," he verified, following her sweeping glance around the now open floor plan. "I wanted to be able to keep an eye on Jack when I was getting his meals ready."

Well, he'd accomplished that. Theo had gone for a caramel-leather sectional in the living area and a massive eat-in kitchen. Since Kim counted six bins of toys, she figured this was an area where Jack played a lot.

"How much grief did Nadia give you about me staying here?" Kim came out and asked as they shrugged off their coats. They placed them on the rack next to the foyer table, and she shifted both her purse and her laptop bag to her shoulder.

The corner of his mouth lifted for just a moment before he sighed. "Some. She knows it's the smart thing to do to have you here though."

Yes, Nadia probably did know that, but it would still sting for her. That reminder gave Kim another flick of annoyance that she hoped she could tamp down before Theo saw it.

She failed.

"I'm stating the obvious, but her reaction bothers me, too," Theo volunteered. He paused a heartbeat. "It bothers me even more that I've accommodated her jealousy for years. I should have tried harder to tamp it down."

Kim nearly said that no tamping would have fixed that, but instead she focused on what Theo hadn't said. Was he wishing he'd pushed Nadia to end this jealousy stuff so he could move on with his personal life?

When their gazes connected, Kim realized she was right. And Theo wanted that moving on to include her. She wanted that as well. Mercy, did she. But the timing was as bad as it could get for them to dive into an actual relationship. Still, she felt the heat slide over her when his gaze lowered to her mouth.

"If we kiss right now, it wouldn't stay just a kiss," she pointed out.

The corner of his mouth lifted again, but this time it was a real smile. A short-lived one, though, followed by a groan of frustration. "True, and I need to go through a whole bunch of reports that have been coming in over the past hour." He tipped his head to the kitchen. "Help yourself to anything in the fridge. There's stuff to make sandwiches."

She wasn't hungry, but it occurred to her they should both eat. If she made some sandwiches, Theo might eat one as well. However, when she went into the kitchen, she spotted something on the counter that had her coming to a stop. There was a stack of file folders, and she recognized the one that was open. Because she had a copy of the same file.

"These are from your parents' murders," she muttered. Since he hadn't been back home since they'd found Faith, it meant he'd been digging into it before he'd even known his sister was alive.

Theo made a sound of agreement and walked closer, looking down at one of the crime scene photos with her. It was a shot of the blood smears on the white-tiled kitchen floor. There'd been no recoverable foot or shoe prints, but the killer had walked through that blood either shortly after committing the murders or else on his way out of the house once he'd had Faith.

"Sometimes in my dreams, I can fix it before it happens," Theo said, his voice tight, and there was regret— oh, so much regret—on his face. "Sometimes, I can stop him."

She echoed his sigh with one of her own because that was true for her as well. But those were rare dreams. Mostly, she got the nightmares.

Kim risked touching his arm with just her finger-tips, and she rubbed gently, hoping it would soothe him in some small way. It did. His eyes were less troubled when he looked at her, but she immediately saw another round of the blasted heat, too. Muttering some profanity, she pulled back her hand because she hadn't lied when she had insisted a kiss wouldn't just stop at a kiss. Her body and mind were primed for Theo, and while she might get to have him down the road, it couldn't be now.

She repeated that to herself several times.

Finally, she forced her gaze off him, and Theo obvi-ously did the same because he motioned to the stairs. "Come on, we can put your things in the guest room."

Kim followed him, trying to ignore the incredible view of his backside as they made their way up the steps. She truly did have a bad case of Theo-itis.

When they reached the top of the stairs, he opened the door of the first room on the right. The room, which was actually a suite with a sitting area and bathroom, didn't disappoint with the décor in varying shades of blue.

"My room is just across the hall," he said.

"So, if I get tempted, I won't have far to go," she blurted out before she realized what she was going to say. Kim so wished she'd just kept her mouth closed, but at least it caused Theo to smile again.

"That works both ways," he reminded her, setting

down her suitcase. "Once you're settled, you really should get something to eat."

He turned, wisely so, as if ready to leave, but his phone rang. Theo told her it was Ava and answered.

"You're on speaker," he informed Ava. "And Kim is with me."

"Good, because this is something you'll both want to hear. Grayson has been doing some digging, and he found something on Greg."

"Is this about his financial troubles?" Theo asked.

"No, this is about something that happened twenty-one years ago, on the day before your parents were murdered."

That got Kim's attention. Obviously, Theo's, too, and she saw his jaw muscles stir. "I'm listening," Theo assured her.

"The day before the murders, Greg was involved in a minor car accident," the deputy explained. "The fender bender happened just two miles from your parents' ranch."

Chapter Eleven

Two miles.

Those two words had repeated through Theo's head for nearly twenty-four hours now. Ever since Ava had told him about the report Grayson had found, proving that Greg had been in the vicinity near the time of the murders and Faith's kidnapping.

That meant Greg had had the means, motive and opportunity to have carried out the crimes.

The problem was Theo hadn't been able to question Greg about it because, according to Duran, Greg had ended up in an ER in San Antonio with a stomach bug. Theo had confirmed the man's visit to the ER, had also confirmed that the ER doctor had advised Greg to isolate for twenty-four hours in case he was contagious.

Maybe Greg was faking, but with Duran fighting the demand for an interview, Theo knew he was going to have to wait a little while longer to get the answers he needed. Still, Greg and Duran couldn't indefinitely put off talking to him, and that's why they'd agreed, finally, to come into the sheriff's office today around eleven.

Two hours from now.

Greg and Duran wouldn't be the only ones in inter-rogation either. Pending the results of the GSR test, Quill would be as well. Rowena was also on the sched-ule. Theo was hoping that by the time of her interview, they'd have the results back from the typewriter confis-cated from her house. Even without that, though, Theo still wanted to know if the woman had had any part in sending those letters to Kim. He was getting conflict-ing stories from Quill and Rowena, and it was time for one or both of them to spill the truth.

Of course, all those interviews meant he'd be going to the sheriff's office. It also meant taking Kim with him since he doubted she'd want to stay at his place while all of their suspects were being questioned. Be-sides, Quill's and Rowena's statements could be rele-vant to the trial that was now only two days away. The trial itself paled, though, in comparison to the danger that Kim, Faith and he were facing, but it was still im-portant because Quill had to pay for what he'd done.

Theo turned toward the movement on the stairs and he got a quick jolt of adrenaline before he convinced his body that it wasn't a threat.

It was Kim.

A different kind of threat, and he got a different kind of jolt. One of the sizzling heat.

Somehow, Theo had managed to stop himself from going to her room the night before, but he wasn't sure he wanted to stop himself from kissing her. He might have done exactly that if she hadn't dropped a dollar bill on the counter next to his mug of coffee.

"I know it's normally a penny for your thoughts," she

said, "but I figured you've got way more than a penny's worth."

"I do," he admitted, and he watched as she went to the coffeepot to help herself to a cup.

Maybe because of all the interviews stacked up, she'd opted not for jeans but black pants and a silver-gray sweater that was almost the same color as her eyes. She also hadn't pulled back her long dark brown hair but instead had it falling onto her shoulders.

"Well?" she asked. "Do I get my dollar's worth on you sharing those thoughts?"

He wouldn't be spilling about this heat or about the way he kept noticing everything about her body. Instead, he focused on the investigation and was sorry there hadn't been a lot of progress in that area.

"Still no ID or anything else on the shooter," Theo relayed. "The lab is working on the typewriter."

She nodded as if that's what she'd expected to hear. "I saw a cruiser pull up earlier in front of the house. Anything wrong?"

"No. I had the deputies drop off a cruiser for us to use. I'm short-staffed because of the protection details at the hospital and Nadia's, and I figured I'd get two of the ranch hands to follow us into town when we have to leave."

"Good idea. Speaking of the hospital, I called Faith this morning. She had a restless night, but she's hoping to be released from the hospital today."

Theo definitely hadn't forgotten about that, and moving Faith to his house was a biggie on his to-do list.

He'd need to time her release, though, for when he was finished with the initial interviews.

"Thanks for calling her," Theo said.

Kim shrugged. "I figured it'd ease some of the awkwardness if Faith and I had talked before she gets thrown into the thick of things."

Awkwardness. Yes, that was the word for it. Even though he knew the woman in the hospital was his sister, Theo was still plenty uneasy about her.

"I didn't mention anything to Faith about Greg being involved in a car accident right before your folks were killed," Kim went on as she drank her coffee. "But I did ask her if she recalled Greg ever talking about Silver Creek or her parents. Not the recent stuff over the memories she was getting back. I wanted to know if it was something he brought up years ago. She said she didn't remember anything like that, but that she'd give it some thought."

Good. If Faith could recall Greg mentioning anything about that, then Theo could maybe use it in the interview. Talking about an incident like that wasn't a crime, but coupled with Greg being in the area around the time of the murders could possibly be enough circumstantial evidence to threaten Greg with an arrest.

"There's plenty of breakfast stuff in the fridge," he offered just as his phone rang. Theo actually smiled when he saw Nadia's name on the screen because he knew this call would be from Jack. His son had gotten into the habit of phoning Theo nearly every morning.

"Daddy," Jack greeted the moment Theo answered the call.

"Good morning, buddy." Theo held back on asking how he was, but he'd listen for any signs of tension in the boy's voice. "What'd you have for breakfast?"

"Marsh-a-mellos," he quickly provided. Definitely no tension. Just happiness and excitement. But Theo was puzzled by the food choice.

"You didn't have marshmallows for breakfast," Nadia corrected in the background. "You got one mini marshmallow for using the potty. You had spinach, eggs and biscuits for breakfast."

"A pink marsh-a-mello," Jack happily added. "Yummy."

Theo smiled again. Maybe the treats would help with the potty training process. "Are you playing with Miss Maya today?" Maya was the nanny, and since Jack wouldn't be going anywhere for security reasons, Theo suspected the nanny would have lots of indoor activities planned.

"Yep," Jack confirmed. "Playin', readin' books, marsh-a-mellos."

"Marshmallows only if you use the potty," Nadia interjected. "And let me talk to your dad when you're done."

Apparently, Jack was done because he muttered a quick "I love you, Daddy," and Theo heard him handing off the phone to Nadia.

"Jack, go read your books over by the sofa," Nadia instructed, and Theo knew she was probably trying to get the boy out of hearing range. "Are you actually going to arrest Rowena?" she demanded a few moments later. "She called here, all upset, saying you had cops search her house and that you were going to lock her up."

Theo sighed. "I'm questioning her in a couple of hours. At this point, I have no plans for an arrest." That would change, though, if he found out that Rowena had been harassing Kim all these years with those letters.

"Did you search her house because of something Quill did?" Nadia pressed.

"Sorry, but I can't get into that with you." Theo didn't want Nadia and Rowena discussing the letters or the typewriter since it could give Rowena opportunity to construct a story that might keep her out of hot water.

Even though Nadia didn't voice her protest of being shut out of this, Theo could practically feel her disapproval coming through the phone line.

"There's a lot of talk about this," Nadia finally said. "Talk of Faith's return, too."

Again, it was what Nadia didn't say, but there was probably talk of Kim staying with him at his place as well. There'd been rumors about Kim and him for years, rumors that they were some kind of star-crossed lovers, and this situation would no doubt bring on more of that kind of talk.

"The deputy's still there with you, right?" Theo asked, already knowing the answer, but he wanted to shift the conversation.

"Yes," Nadia responded after a long pause. Then she paused again. "I have some paperwork I need to do. Jack?" she called out. "It's time to say goodbye to your dad."

Theo heard the sound of running footsteps, and a few

seconds later, his son came on the line. "'Bye, Daddy. You get marsh-a-mellos for me?"

Despite the awkward conversation with Nadia, he had to smile. "I will, and you'll get them when you use the potty. Have a good day, buddy. I'll see you soon."

Theo ended the call, looked up and saw that Kim was smiling, too. "You're a good dad."

He shrugged but was more than pleased with the compliment. "I try to be."

Theo would have added more about how easy Jack made it for him to be a good dad, but Kim moved closer, and she stunned him by brushing a kiss on his cheek. She'd no doubt meant to keep it chaste, but Kim and chaste just didn't go together.

She started to step back, but Theo moved in to return the kiss. Not on the cheek either. He'd been burning for Kim all night, so his mouth landed on hers. He felt the immediate kick of lust that was always there just beneath the surface. Felt the wash of heat go through him.

And he felt the need for a whole lot more.

The day before, Kim had warned him that a kiss between them wouldn't stay just a kiss, and she was so right. There was too much need. Too much…everything, and Theo stepped in even closer so he could deepen the kiss.

She responded with a throaty moan and fumbled around to set her coffee on the counter. He soon learned that was to free up her hands so she could take hold of him and pull him to her. Body to body.

Oh, man. He was toast.

The touching and kissing caused the heat to skyrocket, and as Kim had predicted, things quickly got out of hand. Grappling for position, he turned Kim so that her back landed against the rim of the counter, and he pressed himself to her.

She moaned again, the sound of need and pleasure, and he felt his body pressure him to keep taking more, more, more. Mercy, he wanted more. He wanted Kim. But he had just a shred of logic and sanity left to remind him that the timing for this still sucked.

Theo might have ignored that shred, might have started getting Kim naked, but his phone rang again. His first thought was that it was Jack calling back because he'd forgotten to tell Theo something, but when he was able to focus, it was Ava's name on the screen.

He cursed, and even though Kim didn't voice any profanity, her groan was filled with disappointment— and some shreds of her own logic and sanity. Theo cleared his throat. Tried to clear his head, too, and he answered.

"Please tell me none of our suspects has tried to cancel their interviews," Theo greeted.

"No, just the opposite. Greg and Duran just showed up and asked if they could talk to you earlier than planned. Apparently, they have other business to take care of and wanted to get this out of the way."

Interesting. That shook off some of the mental haze left over from the scalding kiss. Maybe Greg had learned that Ashley was Faith. Or the man could have realized they'd find out about the car accident he'd had in Silver Creek and thought it would make him look like less of a suspect if he got all of that out in the open.

Theo glanced at Kim, silently questioning if she was ready to go. She gave him a nod and went to the front of the house to get her purse and coat.

"Kim and I are on the way," Theo explained to Ava. "I want Kim to observe all the interviews today." No need for him to spell out that Kim had a vested interest in anything and everything that might be said.

"Of course. I'll make sure the camera feed is set up so she can view it in your office."

The camera feed, a replacement for the old two-way glass, was a recent update. It allowed multiple people to watch at once, and in addition to Kim, Theo texted Grayson to have him observe the feed from home. Since Grayson had been the primary investigator of Theo's parents' murders, he would no doubt want to hear what Greg had to say about that car accident.

Theo sent another text to the ranch hands, the ones that Theo had chosen to follow Kim and him to the station. Since the hands were already on guard duty out front, they were waiting in a truck parked behind the cruiser.

Thankfully, it wasn't nearly as cold as it had been the day before, but the wind still had a bite to it. That was yet another reason to hurry inside the cruiser. The main reason, though, was so a sniper wouldn't be given a chance to try to kill them again.

"I don't want you to apologize for that kiss," Kim insisted as they drove away from the ranch. The truck with the hands was right behind them and, despite the conversation that Kim had launched right into, Theo knew they were all keeping watch.

"I wasn't," he assured her and gave her a quick glance to let her know when the opportunity arose, he'd kiss her again. "Once I've arrested the shooter and the danger is over, I also plan on letting Nadia know that I intend to start seeing you. It's long overdue," he tacked onto that.

She made a quick sound of agreement, but Theo knew this was going to cause some conflict with Nadia. No way to avoid that, though, and he was tired of tip-toeing around his ex's feelings when it came to Kim. He wanted to be with Kim and, judging from that kiss, she wanted the same thing.

Theo had to push all such thoughts aside when he pulled to a stop in front of the sheriff's office, but the idea of actually taking Kim on a date was yet another reason for him to plow forward in this investigation and arrest the person who'd fired those shots at them.

The moment they got inside the sheriff's office, Theo spotted Greg and Duran. Even though they'd come in early for the interview, it was obvious they were impatient and maybe even riled that he hadn't been there to accommodate them. Theo didn't accommodate them now either. He spared them both warning glances and ushered Kim into his office.

As expected, Ava was there, and she was setting up the camera feed on Theo's computer. "You want me in the interview with you?" Ava asked him.

Theo shook his head. "Both Rowena and Quill are coming in, and I'd like you to be out here to make sure they don't get into one of their altercations. If Quill makes any wrong move, even a minor one, arrest him."

Ava assured him that she would be happy to do that, and while she showed Kim how to work the camera feed, Theo motioned for Greg and Duran to follow him into the interview room.

"I brought a copy of the medical report for my client's visit to the ER," Duran said as they walked. "Just in case you doubted that he'd been sick."

"I've already verified he was there." But Theo took the report anyway just in case there was anything in it to indicate Greg had faked the illness.

"I also need to tell you about an incident that happened twenty-one years ago," Greg volunteered the moment they stepped into the interview room. "It just didn't occur to me to mention it before now. It has nothing to do with your investigation, but I thought it might come up in a background check, and I didn't want you to jump to the wrong assumption."

Theo held up his hand to stop the man from continuing and read Greg his Miranda rights again just to make sure Duran couldn't squawk later about his client not understanding that he might have been incriminating himself by offering up this info. He also didn't pull back on the flat look he gave Greg because Theo figured it had indeed occurred to the man to perhaps *mention* it before now. Of course, Greg hadn't because it would make him look guilty of some kind of participation in the murders and Faith's kidnapping.

"Twenty-one years ago, my client was involved in a minor vehicular accident near Silver Creek," Duran spoke up once Greg had been Mirandized. "We understand the timing of that accident could make you—"

"Jump to the wrong assumption," Theo interrupted. "Well, I've already jumped." He leveled his stare on Greg to finish what he had to say. "You were in the vicinity of a double murder, home invasion and kidnapping. Added to that, you've admitted to being close friends with the couple who illegally adopted the kidnapped child. In fact, you were engaged to her."

"*Am* engaged," Greg corrected.

Theo didn't respond. He just stared at the man until Greg huffed.

"I still love Ashley, and as far as I know, she's my fiancée," Greg insisted. "Of course, I haven't been able to personally confirm that because you're refusing to let me see her." Duran and he exchanged glances. "Is she still claiming to be your sister?"

"She *is* my sister," Theo said, and he studied both of the men's expressions. No surprise whatsoever for Duran, but there was plenty in Greg's eyes. Surprise, though, could be faked.

"You have proof of that?" Greg wanted to know.

"I do." Theo threw it out there, and then he paused. He wanted Greg to squirm over the possibility that Faith had remembered who she was. And that she could identify him as the man who'd taken her.

Greg did some squirming all right, and Theo was pretty sure that was fear he saw go through the man's eyes. He'd have to quell that fear soon, though, because he didn't want Greg or Duran going after Faith to try to silence her. Still, he could hold off a couple of minutes before he spilled that Faith couldn't identify her kidnapper, and in those minutes maybe Greg would confess to the crimes.

"She's Faith," Greg muttered. He was examining Theo's expression, as well, and that's why Theo kept on his cop's face, which he knew would be hard for Greg to read.

"Ashley... Faith is aware of who she is?" Duran asked.

Theo nodded. Waited. He hoped either Duran or Greg would want to fill the uncomfortable silence with something Theo could use to make an arrest.

"Well," Greg finally said. His breathing was rushed now, and he scrubbed his hand over his face. "She was right after all."

Again, Theo just settled for a nod.

"This means it's even more important that I speak to her," Greg went on. "She'll need help trying to come to terms with this."

"My sister is getting help." Theo kept his voice flat. Kept his intense stare on the man.

"But she'll want to see me," Greg insisted. "I'm sure she's asked to see me."

Theo shook his head. "No, Faith doesn't want to see you."

There. It was like a gauntlet being thrown, and Theo hoped it would cause Greg to verbally explode. It might have done exactly that if Duran hadn't taken hold of his client's arm. Duran gave Greg a squeeze that was no doubt a warning for him to stay quiet.

Greg heeded the warning, but Theo could see him wrestling with the reins he had on his temper. "Faith will want to see me once she's thinking straight. She knows how much I love her." He paused now, his gaze coming back to Theo. "She remembers what happened to her that night your parents were killed?"

Apparently, those minutes of watching Greg squirm were up. "Faith doesn't remember." Theo spelled it out. "Well, she doesn't remember anything other than what she's already told you. She did tell you about the memory flashes she's been having, right?"

"Of course," Greg readily answered. He shook his head and seemed to be frustrated with himself. "I didn't believe her. I thought the flashes were simply things she'd picked up when she was reading all those articles about your parents' murders. She was obsessed with them."

And that brought Theo back to the reason Greg was in the interview room. "Explain why you were near Silver Creek less than twenty-four hours prior to those murders and Faith's kidnapping."

Greg didn't get defensive, nor did he hesitate, which meant he'd already figured out how to put the best spin on this. If there was a best spin, that is. "I was visiting a friend in Wimberly, and I got lost," he stated.

Theo was certain his look turned skeptical. "Wimberly," he repeated. "That's over twenty miles from Silver Creek."

Greg gave a quick nod. "Like I said, I got lost, and it took me a while to find a place so I could turn around."

"I know the area where you had your accident," Theo pointed out. "There have been ranch trails out there for over a hundred years. Plenty of places to turn around."

"Plenty if you're familiar with the area," Duran quickly interjected. "Greg wasn't. He was lost, and his friend's address wasn't showing up on the GPS."

There was a notepad and pen on the table, and Theo slid both toward Greg. "Write down the name and contact info for your friend."

"I don't have it. Uh, I mean I don't know how to get in touch with him." He stopped and huffed. "For Pete's sake, it was twenty-one years ago."

Theo kept staring at him. "Then, write down his name, and I'll contact him to verify you were indeed supposed to visit him that day at that time."

"He didn't know about the visit," Greg insisted. "And after I got lost and went home, I didn't tell him I'd tried to go see him."

"Convenient," Theo muttered. "Write down his name anyway. I'll talk to him and ask if you two had the kind of friendship where you would have just showed up unannounced at his place."

Something went through Greg's eyes. Panic, maybe. Perhaps even fear. And that's when Theo knew the guy was lying about why he'd been on that road near Silver Creek.

It was possible Greg just wanted to say something, anything, that would take him off the suspect list for a double murder. People lied for all sorts of reasons. However, the circumstantial evidence was starting to stack up. It still wasn't enough for a warrant, but after chatting with the friend whose name Greg finally wrote down, Theo might be able to build a case against him.

When Greg passed the notepad with the name back

to him, Theo looked up at the surveillance camera. "Deputy Lawson, contact a man named Jason Pennington who lived in Wimberly twenty-one years ago. I need to speak to him right away."

"Even if Mr. Pennington doesn't remember Greg's account of things," Duran spoke up, "it doesn't mean Greg is lying. He didn't know your parents and had no reason to want them dead."

Yeah, he would have had a reason if Faith had been the target that night. "You were twenty-eight when you had that car accident," Theo continued, not verbally addressing what Duran had said, "and shortly thereafter the Neelys adopted Faith." He left it at that and waited to see Greg's reaction.

Greg shoved back the chair, the metal scraping against the tile floor, and he got to his feet. Apparently, he'd lost the wrestling match with his temper. "I had nothing to do with that. Nothing," he repeated. He looked at Duran as if he expected the lawyer to magically produce some kind of evidence that would make him innocent.

Duran cleared his throat and pinned his attention to Theo. "I'm assuming you have no evidence to indicate Greg's participation in the crimes of twenty-one years ago, or you would have already charged him."

Theo shrugged. "Evidence could come to light. As we speak, I have deputies going over the adoption papers, and they're talking to the Neelys' neighbors and friends. We'll keep digging until we find out who kidnapped my sister and took her to the Neelys." He leaned in, meeting Greg eye to eye. "Because whoever helped with that is also connected to two murders."

Some of the color drained from Greg's face and he eased back down into the chair. "Has Faith said something about the adoption? Has she accused me?" But he didn't wait for Theo to deny it. "Because she could be lying. Faith lies about things, and you can't trust her."

Theo felt the gut punch of emotions that went along with the need to defend and protect his kid sister, even though she was no longer a kid. "Explain what you mean by that," Theo insisted.

Greg opened his mouth, closed it. "Uh, I need to speak privately with my lawyer for a moment. Privately," he emphasized, pointing to the camera.

"I'll turn it off," Theo assured him before he got up and walked out, shutting the door behind him.

Kim was waiting for him in the doorway of his office. "Greg had better not try to put any of the blame on Faith for her own kidnapping," Kim insisted. Obviously, she was feeling a boatload of emotions about Faith, too.

"I won't let him," Theo assured her. He would have added more, but he spotted Rowena walking in.

As usual, the woman looked ready to jump at her own shadow, but Theo had to consider part of that might be an act. Even though Quill wasn't exactly a trustworthy source, Theo had to at least question Rowena about any part she might have had in taunting Kim.

Rowena's gaze zoomed right in on Theo, and she started toward him. "I haven't used that typewriter in years," she insisted. "You can't arrest me for something I didn't do."

"I'm not arresting you," Theo said, and he motioned for her to come into his office.

Rowena, however, stayed put, and she frantically shook her head. "Quill said you were going to arrest me for writing some letters. I haven't. I swear I haven't."

Theo didn't come out and say he was leaning toward believing her. But he was. "Come into my office, and we can talk. For a couple of minutes anyway. I have someone else in Interview, but once I've finished with him, I can take your statement."

"I need you to clear my name," Rowena demanded. Well, it was a demand for her anyway. She didn't raise her voice, but her tone was more adamant than usual. "I saw Quill using that typewriter. I don't know what he typed on it, but it could have been letters."

Yeah, it could have been, and Quill would absolutely do something like that. Theo would need to check the timing, but it was possible the first letter did indeed co-incide with when Kim had started working at the DA's office. With as many run-ins with the law as Quill had had, he would have crossed legal paths with Kim and might have wanted to get back at her for doing her job.

"Sheriff," Theo heard Duran call out. The lawyer rounded the corner and froze.

Rowena froze, too, and her gaze seemed to lock with Duran's. The woman suddenly darted behind Theo.

"Do you two know each other?" Theo asked.

Duran's mouth tightened and he sighed. However, it was Rowena who spoke first.

"Yes, we know each other," the woman muttered, her voice a tangle of nerves and fear. "And I think he might be here to kill me."

Chapter Twelve

Of all the things that Kim had thought Rowena might say, that wasn't one of them. But since the woman was trembling all over, it was obvious she was terrified of the lawyer.

"I have no reason whatsoever to kill you," Duran insisted after he huffed. He definitely wasn't trembling, but he was shooting eye daggers at Rowena.

"But you know each other," Kim pointed out.

"Oh, I know Rowena all right," Duran admitted.

Rowena supplied even more. "Quill worked for him a while back."

Even though *a while back* was plenty vague, Kim's thoughts immediately went to twenty-one years ago. With the rumors of Duran's connections to black market adoptions, Quill would have been a good local source for Duran to find a child for the Neelys.

"When exactly did Quill work for you?" Theo pressed, taking the question right out of Kim's mouth.

Duran muttered a single word of profanity under his breath. "We need to talk."

Kim wanted to curse, as well, and she studied Duran's

body language. He didn't appear to be getting ready to flee the scene. Or to confess that he was a cold-blooded killer. But a need to talk probably meant he had some information or at least some speculation about Theo's parents and Faith's abduction.

"You want to talk with or without your client?" Theo asked.

Duran didn't jump to answer and, after several really long moments, he finally said, "With."

Theo nodded and motioned for them all to follow him to the interview room. Kim didn't stay put. She went with them while she heard Ava call out that she'd start the recording again.

Kim expected Duran to object to that, but he didn't. However, he did go into the interview room ahead of them, and he went straight to Greg and whispered something in his ear. Whatever he said caused Greg's eyes to widen, and he shot Rowena a wary glance.

Or Kim thought it might be wariness. There was something she couldn't quite put her finger on, and whatever it was, Rowena must have been feeling some of it, too, because she dropped back a step.

"Best to get this all out in the open," Duran insisted. "Quill did some part-time work about twenty-plus years ago. Just routine things like tracking down witnesses who might be needed to clear a client's name."

"Hired muscle," Kim quickly provided, earning her a glare from Duran. "Quill's size and attitude make him very intimidating."

"I never used intimidation on a witness," Duran countered. "And I never instructed Quill to do that either." He paused, and it looked as if he was trying to rein in his anger. Or come up with an excuse for hiring a known thug. "I hadn't been practicing law for long then, and I couldn't afford anyone better."

"How'd you know about Quill?" Theo asked. "He's never lived in San Antonio."

"I heard about him through a friend, and he only worked for me a couple of months because I was getting too many complaints about him."

No surprise there. Quill's temper wasn't a recent development.

"You said he worked for you twenty-plus years ago," Theo stated. "Specifically, was that twenty-one years ago?"

Now, Duran dragged in a lengthy breath. "Yes." And that was all he said for a long time. "You want to know if Quill could have had some part in your parents' murders and your sister's disappearance, and I have to say it's possible."

"Quill wouldn't have done that," Rowena spoke up. She frantically shook her head. "He wouldn't have killed your parents."

Since the woman didn't address the second part of that, Kim did. "But he might have taken Faith so she could be adopted."

Rowena went sheet-white. "No," she muttered. "No." But everyone in the room had to have heard the doubt in her voice.

"I did the adoption paperwork for the Neelys," Duran went on, "but I didn't get the child for them. There'd be no need for me to do that. I had connections to adoption agencies, and I could have found them a child without having to kidnap one."

"Maybe," Kim agreed. "But you might not have been able to find them a child who looked so much like their late daughter."

That turned Duran's jaw to iron. "I didn't have anything to do with getting them that girl."

"Neither did I," Greg interjected.

Kim was certain Theo's skeptical look matched hers. "Then why were you so close to Silver Creek when Faith was taken?" Theo fired back.

"I've already told you…" Greg stopped, groaned. "I was seeing someone in Silver Creek. A married woman, and I was going to her house."

"So, you lied earlier when you said you were visiting a friend and got lost," Kim pointed out.

"Yes, I lied." There was no remorse in the man's tone, only defiance. "She's still married, still lives here, and I don't want to make things hard for her by bringing up something that happened a lifetime ago. We broke off things shortly after the car accident," Greg added.

Theo opened his mouth and Kim knew he was about to demand the name of the woman, but he stopped. Turned. And his attention landed on Rowena. One look at her, and Kim saw the guilt.

Oh, mercy.

"You had an affair with Greg?" Theo came out and asked.

Rowena shook her head as tears sprang to her eyes, and it didn't take long for the tears to turn to a full sob.

"It was a mistake, and I don't want Quill to ever find out about it."

"Quill would kill both of us," Greg added to that. "Even after all this time, he'd kill both of us."

If Quill got the chance, yes, he would. And that's why Kim wanted to sigh. Because all of these statements had to become part of the investigative reports. *Had to.* Rowena and Greg would have to be questioned, would be asked to provide proof they'd been together so it could either corroborate or disprove Greg's claim of innocence in the murders and kidnapping.

And word of that could get back to Quill.

"Deputy Lawson," Theo said looking at the camera, "have Quill brought in right away."

"He'll kill us," Rowena echoed with the tears streaming down her cheeks. "The affair with Greg was a mistake, but Quill won't ever be able to forgive me for it."

"I want you in protective custody," Theo told the woman.

That was a wise move, especially considering that Quill would get some fuel for his temper once he found out he was now connected to the murder of Theo's parents. Even though it was a much lesser charge, Quill would soon find out that he was the most likely suspect for sending those taunting letters. That in itself wouldn't be a serious charge, but all of this was adding up, and it wasn't adding up in Quill's favor.

"You mean like go to a safe house?" Rowena asked just as Greg said, "I need that, too."

Theo ignored Greg and focused on Rowena. "Yes, a

safe house, or I can ask the marshals to provide security if you want to stay at your own place."

"I don't want to be at my place where Quill can find me," Rowena answered in a whisper.

"I need a safe house," Greg demanded, his voice a lot louder this time.

"Hush," Theo warned him. "You're not going anywhere until you've made a full and correct statement as to your whereabouts at the time of the murders and kidnapping. Lie again," Theo said, his voice hardening even more, "and I'll toss you in a cell."

"My client will give you an honest account of that time," Duran spoke up.

There was some hardness in his voice, too. Maybe because he was trying to save Greg from being charged with murder. Maybe because the lawyer was just trying to put a quick end to this so he could get out of there without having to answer too many more questions about Faith's adoption.

But there would be questions.

Hard ones. And every word of the adoption Duran had done for the Neelys would be examined.

Kim turned when she heard the footsteps in the hall. Theo did, too, and he was obviously primed for a threat or attack because he moved his hand to his gun. No threat though. It was Ava. She motioned for Kim and Theo to step out into the hall with her.

"Gage just called from the hospital," Ava said, keeping her voice at a whisper. "Faith is ready to be released, and she's asking for the two of you to pick her up right away. She says she's scared and doesn't want to be there any longer."

Theo groaned softly and dragged his hand over his face. The timing wasn't exactly ideal, and both of them knew that.

"Jesse and Nelline are in the squad room, so let us mop up here for you," Ava volunteered. "Jesse can help with the interviews, and Nelline can go with you to the hospital."

"But Quill needs to be brought in," Theo reminded her.

Ava nodded. "I just tried to call him, and he's not answering his phone, but I'll arrange for another deputy to go out to his place, and if he's there, he'll be brought in. After I call the marshals for a safe house, or two—" she gave Greg a quick glance "—I can take the statements of these three while you go deal with your sister."

"I'll call the marshals." Theo compromised after glancing at his watch. "One safe house for now for Rowena. They'll move fast on that because of Quill's history with her. Did Quill get his car from Kim's?"

Ava nodded. Then, she sighed, and Kim knew why. That meant Quill could be anywhere right now since he had a vehicle.

"We got back the results from Quill's GSR," Ava added. "Negative."

Theo huffed. A positive would have been grounds for an arrest, but a negative meant pretty much nothing. Quill could have still fired those shots and managed not to get an GSR on him if he'd worn gloves or used a rifle.

"After you've given your statement to Deputy Lawson," Theo said, turning toward Greg, "she'll decide if charges will be filed against you. If not," Theo continued over Greg's howl of protest, "then I'll see about a safe house for you, too."

Duran put his hand on Greg's arm, but he aimed his glare at Theo. "Since it'd be a travesty if my client were to be charged with anything, I believe he'll soon be leaving Silver Creek. I have a place where he can stay and be safe in case Quill decides to, well, be Quill."

Since Theo stayed put, Kim figured he was having a debate with himself about all of these arrangements. But there was also the fact that his sister was waiting for him to come and get her. A sister who was terrified but might also be able to provide them answers as to what had happened the night of her abduction. It was possible that, with some questioning, Faith would be able to clue them into the identity of the person who'd taken her. That, in turn, could help them arrest the person who was trying to kill them now.

Because Kim was convinced it was the same person.

Or someone connected to the same person.

That didn't rule out any of their suspects. Quill, Greg or Duran. Heck, it didn't rule out Rowena assisting, either, especially if she'd been romantically involved with Greg at the time. If Greg had asked his lover to help, she might have done it even though Kim couldn't see the waif-like Rowena hauling an eight-year-old child down a flight of stairs and out of the house.

Theo finally got moving after telling Ava to call him immediately if Quill showed up or if Duran and Greg gave her any trouble with the rest of the interviews.

Considering that Duran and Greg both wanted to get the heck out of there, they might cooperate. Of course, there were no guarantees they'd tell the truth either.

"I wish I had enough to hold Greg and Duran," Theo muttered as they made their way to the front of the police station.

So did she, but Kim couldn't imagine getting an arrest warrant with what they had. They needed physical evidence or a confession to add to the circumstantial.

As Ava had said, Jesse was in the squad room, and he was on the phone. "Trying to track down Quill," he informed them.

Theo gave him a nod of approval and went to the door where Nelline was waiting to drive with them to the hospital. Since Theo likely wouldn't want to bring Faith back to the sheriff's office, that meant they'd be going straight to his place where he might get a chance to listen to the interviews if they were still going on by then.

"How many lies do you think Greg has told us?" Theo muttered after they'd all gotten in the cruiser.

"Well, he lied about why he was so near Silver Creek, but I think that's just the tip of the iceberg," Kim said. "At minimum, I believe he also knew the Neelys had illegally adopted Faith. His association with Quill and Duran likely means he was involved with what happened, even if it was some level of accessory after the fact."

Theo made a quick sound of agreement. "They could all be in on it, and if so, all of them will pay. I'll make sure of it."

Even after all these years, his need for justice hadn't waned one bit. Neither had hers, and Kim was hoping that if they finally found the person or persons responsible, she might be able to get through a week without having nightmares.

As with their other trip to the hospital, Nelline parked right by the ER doors. According to one of the updates Theo had gotten yesterday, the crime scene tape had been removed shortly after the bomb squad had cleared the building, and with it gone, there were no signs of the shooting that'd happened nearly twenty-four hours earlier. But Theo and Kim were well aware of it and that's why they didn't waste any time being outside.

They went straight to Faith's room, where a reserve deputy, Mike Gonzales, was standing guard. When they went in, they found Faith not in the bed but pacing the small room. She wasn't near the windows but rather using the very narrow space between the bed and the bathroom.

"You came," she blurted out. The relief eased some of the tight muscles in her face. "I was worried you wouldn't."

"Of course, we came." Theo went to her and pulled her into a hug. Not exactly a natural one since both of them looked a little stiff. Still, it was a hug, and Kim was hoping it would soothe them some.

"I'm going to your house, right?" Faith asked. "And you'll be there?" she added to Kim.

Kim made a quick sound of agreement and gave Faith her own hug once Theo had stepped back. "I'll stay as long as Theo and you want me there." That, Kim was hoping, would be until they'd caught the killer.

Faith let out a quick breath of relief. "Good. And Greg won't be able to see me, right?"

"Right," Theo confirmed. "Greg and Duran are at the sheriff's office right now." He paused, no doubt trying to decide how much to tell her. Faith didn't look exactly steady, and none of the recent revelations was going to help with that unsteadiness. "Greg admitted to being near Silver Creek at the time of your kidnapping. Is there any chance he was the one who carried you out of the house that night?"

Faith made a strangled sound and pressed her hand to her heart as if to steady it. "Greg wouldn't have done that." She paused, her breath shuddering. "Would he?" She repeated that while catching on to Theo's arm.

He looked his sister straight in the eyes. "I'm not sure, but it's possible."

Faith began to frantically shake her head. "If it'd been him, I would have known. I would have felt... something." She stopped again, and this time pressed her fingertips to her trembling mouth. "Oh, God."

Kim figured that Faith's thoughts were whirling right now. Whirling with possibilities she didn't want to accept. After all, she had gotten engaged to Greg, so that meant she had at least some feelings for him. Had maybe even loved him. If he'd been the one who'd kidnapped her, then this was the worst kind of betrayal. Added to that, it also meant Greg might have had some part in her parents' murders.

"All this time I trusted him," Faith muttered, and she sank down on the foot of the bed. The tears pooled in her eyes. Eyes that she turned up to Theo. "I have to tell you something. Something you aren't going to like. God, Theo. I'm so sorry."

Kim felt the whirl of her own emotions and she definitely didn't like the sound of what Faith had just said. Judging from the glance Theo gave her, neither did he.

"What are you sorry about?" Theo asked.

Faith didn't give them a quick answer. She continued to shake her head and then buried her face in her hands. Kim moved toward her, to try to settle her enough so she could explain that apology.

But the sound stopped her.

One second the room was quiet and the next second there was a deafening blast. The window shattered and glass spewed through the room. Kim had just a split-second awareness of what was happening.

Someone had just fired a shot at them.

She moved fast, but Theo was faster. He caught onto both Faith and her and dragged them to the floor just as the next shot came. It slammed into the wall near the door.

"What the hell?" she heard Deputy Gonzales shout.

"Stay down," Theo warned the deputy when he opened the door.

The deputy did, but he dropped to the floor and crawled toward them while Theo shoved Faith and Kim under the bed. No way would the bedding and frame stop bullets, but for the gunman to get to them, he'd have to change the angle of the shots.

"Is Greg doing this?" Faith blurted.

Kim seriously doubted it. If Duran and he had already left the sheriff's office, Ava would have no doubt alerted Theo, and he hadn't gotten any calls or texts since they'd arrived in Faith's room.

More shots came. Not a single bullet this time. But a barrage of gunfire that Kim could hear blasting through what was left of the window. Maybe, just maybe, none of the shots would go through the wall and hit any of the staff or patients.

Kim heard the deputy call for backup and inform Dispatch there was an active shooter. That meant responding officers wouldn't be able to just charge in and get this snake who was trying to kill them. It could be a slow process with them at the mercy of someone who wanted them dead.

Dead.

And this time, he just might succeed.

She cursed the wave of flashbacks. Cursed her too-fast breathing and heartbeat. The panic was crawling its way through her. Through Faith, too. Faith latched onto her, burying her face against Kim's shoulder, and Kim thought the woman might be on the verge of a full-fledged panic attack.

"It'll be okay," Kim murmured to her. Maybe a lie, but if she couldn't get Faith at least somewhat level, the woman might try to run.

"Put out an alert for everyone to get inside and stay away from the windows," Theo instructed Mike. "I want the entire block cordoned off."

The deputy rattled off those instructions to whoever

was on the other end of the phone line. "Done," he told Theo. "Do you see the guy?"

That's when Kim realized that Theo had moved. He was no longer by the bed but had levered himself up to peer out the window. She nearly shouted for him to get back, but a bullet accomplished that. There was another barrage of gunfire, and Theo dropped back down to the floor.

"The shots are coming from the west," Theo explained to the deputy. "My guess is the rooftop of one of the buildings up the street."

Mike relayed that to the responder he had on the line, but he had to repeat it several times because of the gunfire drowning him out. "Nelline's driving the cruiser back there now. She won't get out, but she's hoping the approaching siren will spook him and cause him to run."

Good. That might be enough to put an end to this nightmare, but Kim prayed it wouldn't cause the guy to turn the shots on Nelline. The cruiser was bullet resistant. That didn't mean those shots couldn't get through.

More glass came flying through the room and crashed onto the floor when the gunman managed to fire through another portion of the window. And that caused Kim's heart to sink. Because it likely meant the guy was on the move. Looking for the right angle to take the kill shots.

In the hallway, Kim could hear the shouts and the sounds of panic, but even with that and the gunfire, she heard the welcome sound of sirens. Maybe the shooter heard them, too, or maybe Nelline had managed to get close enough to him that he knew he had to get the heck out of there. Either way, the shots stopped.

Kim held her breath, waiting and praying, but as the seconds passed, there was no more gunfire.

Theo peered under the bed at them. "Are you both okay?"

Not trusting her voice yet, Kim went with a nod. Neither Faith nor she had been physically hurt and, considering the sheer number of shots that had been fired, that was somewhat of a miracle.

"Are you all right?" Kim asked him though, thankfully, she couldn't see any injuries.

Theo nodded as well. "I need you both to stay put while I make sure there are no injuries in the hall."

Injuries, yes. Perhaps even deaths if bystanders had been hit. It twisted at her to think someone else could have paid the ultimate price because a gunman had been reckless enough to fire into a building crammed with people.

"I need to know if Greg did this," Faith muttered, and Kim hadn't thought it possible, but the woman began to tremble even more.

"I'll find out who's responsible," Theo said like a promise. He started to move away when Faith took hold of his arm.

"I…" Faith stopped, a broken sob tearing from her throat. "I might be responsible. This might all be because of me."

Kim was about to assure her that it wasn't her fault, but she heard something in Faith's voice. Something more than the panic and the fear.

Regret, maybe.

"Theo, I'm so sorry," Faith blurted out. "I've been lying to you about so many things."

Chapter Thirteen

Even with the adrenaline slamming through him and the urgent need to go after the shooter, Theo had no trouble hearing what Faith had just said.

I've been lying to you about so many things.

Hell. That was not what he wanted this woman to say, and he immediately recalled Greg telling him that Faith was a liar.

If this was actually Faith, that is.

"Did you somehow fake the fingerprint match so it would look like you're my sister?" he snarled.

Faith flinched, maybe at his harsh tone or maybe because she was so stunned by his accusation. "No," she said, and she repeated it several times. "I really am Faith. I didn't lie about that."

That didn't do much to soothe his anger. Heck, he wasn't even sure he could believe her. It sickened him to think this woman was playing some kind of mind games with them.

"Theo," Kim murmured, her voice soft and soothing. It was a serious contrast to his own tone. "We should go to another room. It's not safe for us to be in here with the windows."

He certainly hadn't forgotten about the shot-out windows. Or the cold winter air slamming through them. Or the fact there was a shooter out there somewhere who would kill them if he got the chance.

"Nelline's in pursuit of the shooter," Mike relayed to Theo. "Not alone. She's got backup."

Good. Maybe they'd be able to catch the SOB. While Theo was hoping, he added a hope that there wouldn't be any injuries. To get started on checking that, and to move Faith and Kim, he motioned toward the door. It was riddled with bullet holes but was still closed and in the frame.

"We'll need to crawl out of here so we can stay out of the line of fire from the windows," he explained. "Be careful of the glass."

There was so much of it spewed across the floor, it was hard to avoid it, but Kim started inching out from under the bed. When Faith didn't budge, Kim caught onto the woman and pulled her along with her.

"I'm so sorry," Faith kept muttering.

Theo shut her out. Shut out what exactly she'd lied about. He was the sheriff, and right now, he had a job to do.

"Come with us," Theo told Mike. "Secure the hall and start checking for casualties and injuries. I also want updates on Nelline. Make sure she has all the backup we can give her."

Mike followed orders as they all made their way across the room. Once Theo reached the door, he opened it a couple of inches and looked out to see a welcome sight.

Gage was there.

"I was coming to relieve Mike," Gage said, sparing them a glance. He had his weapon drawn, his back pressed against the wall, and he was volleying his attention to both ends of the hall. No doubt looking for the shooter in case he'd managed to make his way into the hospital. "Are all of you okay?"

"We're not hurt," Theo settled for saying. Thankfully, Gage didn't appear to be hurt either, and Theo didn't see any other wounded.

Theo led the others out of the room while he, too, had his gun drawn. When he didn't see any signs of a threat, he took Kim and Faith to a small alcove where there were vending machines. There were no windows there, but he had to make sure the gunman didn't try to get at them some other way.

"No reports of injuries," Mike called out to him. "Since Gage is here, I'll start securing the entrances and exits while I get a status report on Nelline."

Theo thanked him and turned first to Kim. Just to see for himself that she hadn't been hurt. There was a tear on the sleeve of her coat and he realized it'd been made by either flying glass or a bullet. That definitely didn't ease the hard knot in his stomach. He'd come damn close to losing her.

"I'm okay," Kim assured him. Probably because she could see the worry and regret on his face.

Both emotions were there. Regret that he hadn't been able to stop this attack and worry that there might be another one if the gunman wasn't captured. Even then, that might not put an end to it because it was entirely possible the shooter had been a hired gun. No way could Greg or Duran have gotten in place so quickly to do this.

And that left Quill.

Yes, he definitely could have been in place, and that's why questioning the man was a high priority. For now, though, the priority was catching the gunman and keeping everyone safe. However, he also wanted answers, and while this wasn't an ideal time to get them, they also couldn't go anywhere.

"Start talking," Theo demanded, staring directly into Faith's eyes.

She was crying, not quietly, either, but with a steady stream of tears and quick jerks of breath. "I really am your sister. I swear, I didn't lie about that." She stopped and clearly tried to calm herself down so she could continue. It didn't work. "I told you I found the birth certificate for the Neelys' daughter, Ashley, and that's when I got suspicious about my adoption. But I found it before then." Another pause, followed by a sob. "About a year ago."

Theo latched right onto the timing of that. "The Neelys were alive then. You would have been able to ask them about the details of the adoption and how it was you ended up with them."

She nodded. "I did. I asked them a lot of questions, and I could tell this wasn't something they wanted to talk about. They got upset when I pressed, so I spoke to Greg since he would have been around when I was adopted."

"Greg got you for the Neelys?" Theo asked bluntly.

Faith's head whipped up and she shook it. "No." But she stopped. "Maybe. If he did, though, he's never admitted anything about it to me. In fact, after doing some research on our parents' murders, Greg said that he believed you had been the one to kill them."

Theo felt as if she'd punched him, hard, and the breath seemed to swoosh out of his body. Not the anger though. Definitely not that. It riled him to the bone that someone would believe he'd had any part in the killings.

"Why did Greg think that?" Kim asked. Good thing, too, because Theo definitely wanted to know the answer but wasn't sure he could speak just yet.

"Like I said, he'd done a lot of research, and he claimed he'd spoken to some people in Silver Creek who thought Theo might have argued with our parents and things escalated from there."

"That didn't happen," Theo managed to snarl.

"It didn't," Kim confirmed. "Theo was twelve years old. A kid, just like us. And he loved your parents. Added to that, there's no way he kidnapped you. Did Greg have an explanation as to how Theo would have managed that?"

Faith groaned and squeezed her eyes shut a moment. "Greg said it was probably one of Theo's friends who carried me away."

Again, Theo had to tamp down the anger. Hard to do since it had gone bone-deep. "Again, why would I have done that?"

Faith wasn't so quick to answer, and she shook her head. "I was gullible, and Greg convinced me that you wanted me out of the way so you could inherit our family's ranch."

"Greg must have been very persuasive," Theo said, his voice both an accusation and a warning. A warning because Greg was going to pay for filling Faith's head with these awful lies.

"He was," Faith confirmed. "He had what looked like police reports where the cops said they thought you might have been involved but couldn't prove it."

"I've gone over all the reports many times," Kim interjected. "So have plenty of other people, and there's absolutely nothing in them about Theo participating in the crimes in any way."

And that meant Theo could charge Greg with creating a false police report. Probably obstruction of justice, too. It might not lead to any real jail time, but it was a start.

"So, what motive did Greg have for telling you these lies?" Kim asked, but she didn't wait for Faith to answer. "I'm guessing he wanted you to come back to Silver Creek, confront Theo and get your share of the inheritance?"

Bingo. Theo could tell from the shame passing through Faith's eyes that it had gone down that way. And Greg's motive would have been to get his hands on her money to pay off his debts.

"Greg said I had a right to the money," Faith continued a moment later. "A right, too, to put away the person who murdered my parents. He just kept pressing, just kept saying I could right an old wrong." She stopped, groaned, and pressed her hands to both sides of her head. "And that all got mixed up with the grief I was feeling because of the Neelys' dying. I loved them, they'd been good to me, and they were dead."

Theo was definitely listening to her, but he was also keeping an ear to what was going on around them. No sounds of gunfire, but the chatter told him there was a lot of movement to make sure everyone was secure.

"If Greg wanted you to return to Silver Creek to get the money, then why would he insist to us that you weren't Faith?" Kim asked.

Faith shook her head. "I'm not sure. Maybe because he thought you'd arrest him if you found out that he'd put me up to this."

It probably wasn't smart for Theo to believe her, but heaven help him, he did. Well, he believed the parts about Greg pushing Faith to return so she could get the money. That said, the woman might know more than she was saying about her return to Silver Creek.

"You said you had a breakdown after the Neelys were killed," Theo reminded her. "Is it possible Greg pushed you to that breakdown? Maybe even gave you some kind of medication to make you believe you were losing your mind?"

Faith opened her mouth, and Theo was certain she was about to say, *No, that wasn't possible.* But he watched as she worked through the facts. And the fact was he hadn't killed their parents, he hadn't kidnapped her.

But Greg could have done both of those things.

"Oh, God," Faith murmured, and she buried her face against Kim's shoulder while she began to sob again.

Theo wasn't immune to those tears, and he could see

his sister was hurting, but he wasn't done yet with getting those answers he so desperately needed. "Who took you from the house the night our parents were killed?"

"I don't know." Faith lifted her head so she could look him straight in the eyes. "That's the truth. And yes, it could have been Greg."

"Or his lawyer, Duran?" Kim pushed.

Faith stayed quiet a moment, obviously processing that, and she nodded. "He could have done it."

"How about a man named Quill Odell?" Theo asked. "Did you ever hear Greg, Duran or the Neelys mention him?"

Her forehead bunched up while she gave that some thought. "No. Is he a suspect?"

Oh yeah. Not just for the murders and kidnapping but also for the two shootings. If Quill had been the one to kidnap Faith, no way would he want her to stay alive to be able to ID him.

Theo's phone buzzed, and even though he wanted to continue this line of questioning, he knew it was a call he had to take.

"First of all, there have been no reported injuries. But Nelline saw a man with a rifle running in the alley behind the hardware store, and she called out for him to stop," Ava immediately said. "She identified herself, ordered him to stop, and when he turned and took aim at her, she fired."

Hell. All of that had gone on while he'd been here tucked away in the hospital. "What happened?" Theo couldn't ask fast enough.

"Nelline is fine. He shot at her but missed. She believes she hit him, but he still managed to run away. Should I call in the Rangers to assist?"

It would take too long, maybe an hour or more, for the Rangers to send someone out. "No, I'll call Silver Creek Ranch and get us some help."

There were enough lawmen, retired lawmen and ranch hands who could be temporarily deputized, and Grayson could have a team in place in a fraction of the time it would take the Rangers to respond.

"Are Greg and Duran still at the sheriff's office?" Theo asked the deputy.

"They are. They're in the interview room, and when I got reports of a shooting, I warned them to stay put. So far, they have. Rowena, too."

"Good. Make sure word gets out for everyone to stay inside," Theo instructed Ava. "And keep me posted," he added.

He ended the call with the deputy so he could phone Grayson. As expected, Grayson assured him that he and others would be right there to start the search for the gunman.

"Is Nelline okay?" Kim asked Theo the moment he put his phone away.

"She is. Ava said there have been no reported injuries." Theo took a breath of relief over that. Of course, someone could still be hurt, someone who hadn't been able to let anyone know they'd been injured, but for now, the gunman hadn't managed to claim another target. "Nelline believes she shot the guy as he was running away."

Kim seemed to take a breath of relief, too, and she

gave a satisfied nod. "I hope there's a trail of blood to follow."

Theo hoped the same, but he very much wanted the guy alive. Dead men couldn't give him those answers he needed.

"You really believe Greg or Duran could have hired this gunman," Faith said, drawing his attention back to her.

He settled for a nod, as well, because unless it'd been Quill firing those shots, then the most likely scenario was that Greg, Duran or both had paid someone to do their dirty work.

His nod caused Faith's mouth to tremble again, and more tears came. "Greg could have done this if he thought I was going to tell you the truth about why I came here."

Maybe, but if Greg was responsible for these attacks, then he had a lot more at stake than Theo learning why his sister had returned. Greg could want her dead so he wouldn't be facing murder charges.

"I'll leave Silver Creek," Faith said, her words as shaky as the rest of her. "You won't want me near you now that you know the truth."

He wasn't especially happy with a sister who'd not only thought he was a killer but had returned to try to make him pay for that. Still, he couldn't let her go while someone out there wanted her dead.

"You can still stay at my place," he said.

Faith started shaking her head. "No. I can't do that to you. Not when you're obviously disgusted with me."

Theo hadn't known the disgust was showing, but

apparently he hadn't been able to hide it. Except it was more disappointment than disgust. And he'd have to get over it. Yeah, Faith had screwed up by believing and trusting Greg, but it was also possible the man had manipulated her in some way. Kim could have been right about Greg having used some kind of drugs on Faith.

"Is there a hotel or inn?" Faith asked him. "Or maybe I can stay at the police station? Just please don't make me stay here at the hospital. Not after what just happened."

Theo groaned then he sighed. "I'll take Kim and you to my place as planned."

Faith looked at Kim, no doubt to take note of her expression, to see if there was disgust or disappointment.

But Kim gave her a reassuring nod. "You'll be safe at Theo's," she said.

Theo certainly hoped that was true because, hell's bells, there'd been enough shooting and danger. He needed to have both Kim and Faith protected so he could dive into this investigation and find the person or persons responsible.

His phone rang again, and he answered it right away when he saw it was from Ava. "Please tell me you have good news," Theo greeted.

Ava made a sound that could have meant anything. "We have several witnesses who reported seeing Quill in the area at the time of the shooting."

Hell. "And I don't suppose he's answering his phone."

"Nope," Ava verified. "But as soon as someone is available, I'll dispatch them to his house." She paused a moment. "We'll be able to arrest Quill since the lab results just came in and the typewriter is a match to the letters that Kim's been receiving."

Good. They wouldn't necessarily be able to charge Quill with the two shootings or anything to do with what happened twenty-one years ago, but holding him on the letters would get him off the streets. It should be enough to have his bail revoked.

"I'll have to get back to you," Theo told Ava when his phone dinged. "Nelline's calling."

He very much wanted to hear what the deputy had to say so he immediately switched calls. "Are you okay?" Theo asked her.

"I am. Not our gunman though." Nelline muttered some profanity. "We just found him one block up from the hardware store. I'm sorry, Theo, but he's dead."

Chapter Fourteen

Kim felt both exhausted and on pins and needles. That was often the case with an adrenaline crash, and she was indeed dealing with the aftereffects of that slam of adrenaline she'd gotten during the shooting.

Theo was dealing with it, as well, but unlike her, he couldn't go on autopilot. He was running a full-scale investigation, one that might finally catch his parents' killer. Of course, that *finally* couldn't come soon enough since whoever had hired the shooter might come after them again.

As they'd done on their other trips since the attacks had started, they hurried from the cruiser and into Theo's house. What was different this time was that Faith was with them, and instead of Nelline, Mike had driven them. Along with Theo's three ranch hands doing guard duty, Mike would have the next four-hour shift in the cruiser before being relieved by another deputy.

The moment the door was closed, Theo engaged the security system and then continued his call. Over the past seven hours since the shooting, there'd been a lot of calls. So many updates.

And some disappointing news.

For starters, the dead gunman—a thug who'd been immediately identified as Donnie Barker, a man with a mile-long criminal record along with a drug problem. Not a good combination, but Kim suspected the man's need for drugs had helped in him not being able to put bullets in Theo, Faith or her.

Of course, the question now was who'd hired Donnie, but judging from the updates Theo had been getting while they'd been holed up at the hospital and then the sheriff's office, there was no immediate money trail that led from Donnie to any of their suspects. There was enough circumstantial evidence to get a warrant to look at the financials of all three—Quill, Greg and Duran— but that kind of search took time. Added to that, Duran didn't seem careless enough not to cover his tracks.

"I want the tails to continue on Duran and Greg," she heard Theo tell Ava. The deputy had to be worn out, as they were, but Kim figured Ava wouldn't stop until her boss was out of danger. "Also, set the Rangers on Quill. He's on bail and can't just disappear like this."

There was plenty of frustration in Theo's voice, and Kim was right there with him. The fact that Quill hadn't surfaced made him look guilty.

Then again, he could be dead.

If Greg or Duran had used the man to do their bidding, they could have eliminated him. Yes, even with tails watching them, they could have managed it with a phone call to another hired thug.

Since Theo was still on the phone and Faith was looking very much like a fish out of water and ready to drop where she stood, Kim took hold of her hand and led her to the guest room that she'd used the night before. There were probably other guest rooms in the huge house, but this one was convenient, and she wanted Faith away from the constant barrage of updates that were no doubt reminders of how close they'd come to dying. Again.

"Theo doesn't want me here," Faith muttered. She paused in the doorway of the guest room and glanced around. "Not after I lied to him." She turned to Kim. "I'm so sorry I did that. So sorry for all the pain I've caused."

Kim decided to cut the woman a break. "Hey, you've been through a lot, and Theo might be uncomfortable with the way you went about coming here, but he wants what's best for you."

Since Faith wasn't budging from the doorway and they had some time while Theo was on the phone, Kim went with trying to get some facts about Faith's arrival in Silver Creek.

"Now that you've had some time to rethink things— did you tell us the truth about what happened at the hospital in San Antonio?" Kim asked.

Faith practically snapped toward her. "Yes. I had a breakdown, and I've been mulling over what you said about maybe being drugged. The hospital did a tox screen on me when I checked in, and there were some sleeping pills in my blood. I don't remember taking anything like that, but I blew it off. I just figured I was so out of it that I forgot what I'd done."

Sleeping pills. Depending on the type of medication

and the dosage, it could have made Faith groggy enough to forget things she might now be remembering. But if Greg had given her those pills, there's no way he would have wanted her to check into a hospital where she could get help in reclaiming her childhood memories.

"You also told us the truth about why you left the hospital?" Kim pressed. "Because you thought you saw the killer?"

"I did," Faith insisted. She stopped, though, and shook her head. "Things are still fuzzy, but I remember Greg came to see me to take me home. He didn't want me to stay there at the hospital. I refused to leave with him, but after he left, I saw the shadow. Or something. I thought someone was trying to kill me, so I ran away and came to Silver Creek."

Kim thought about that for a moment. "Did you eat or drink anything while Greg was there?"

"Yes," Faith told her. "Greg brought me a BLT from my favorite deli." Her eyes widened. "Do you think he drugged it?"

"Possibly. Something caused the fuzziness." No way to prove it though, but there were other things that might link back to Greg. "How'd you get to Silver Creek?"

Her face brightened a little, the way a student's would when they knew the right answer. "I remembered that last night. I used an Uber. I didn't go to Theo, though, because of what Greg had said about him being a killer."

That made sense. Well, it made sense if you'd been drugged and lied to. "Why go to my house? How did you even know where I lived?"

"I found it when I was researching. It's not hard to

access tax records, and you were listed as the owner of the property." Faith paused and tapped the center of her forehead. She was obviously trying to recall something. "On the drive, my head started hurting, and I got really dizzy. And confused. I had the driver let me out just up the road from your place so I could try to decide if I should go see you or not."

"You ended up in my barn," Kim reminded her. "And someone had followed you. Greg, maybe." But it could have been Duran or Quill as well. If either of them had been worried about what Faith might remember, they could have been keeping tabs on her and known when she'd left the hospital in San Antonio.

"Yes, Greg maybe," Faith muttered, her words a little slurred now. Not from drugs this time but from sheer exhaustion.

"Why don't you lie down and get some rest?" Kim motioned toward the bed. "Theo will be tied up for a while, and you should try to take a nap."

Kim thought maybe Faith would protest doing that, but as testament to just how exhausted she was, she made her way to the bed and dropped down on it. She kicked off her shoes and pulled the cover over her.

And that's how Theo found her when he finally joined Kim in the hall.

One look at his face and Kim knew he was bone-tired. That's why she reached out and pulled him into a hug. She'd intended for it to be short and sweet. A gesture of what she hoped would be comfort, but it lingered on. And on. With the heat from his body seeping into her.

"You look like you needed that," she said when she finally eased back and faced him.

"I do. Especially from you." He brushed his mouth over hers. "I needed that, too."

Kim managed a smile. And felt the slam of heat from what was barely a kiss. Then again, any kiss from Theo packed a punch. A punch that she needed to put aside and focus on what he'd learned.

"Faith and I talked. I have a lot to fill you in on. Nothing that will help us find a killer," she quickly added. "Any updates that will help us find who's doing this?"

He shook his head. "More like stonewalls and road-blocks. Duran is fighting the warrant to go through his financials. Quill is nowhere to be found, and Greg is either holed up in his house in San Antonio or else he's managed to sneak out."

That shot some alarm through her. She nearly asked—could he do that?—but she knew the answer was yes. Suspects slipped surveillance all the time.

Theo must have seen the alarm because he touched her cheek, brushing aside a strand of hair that'd landed there. "If Greg is the killer, he didn't do his dirty work this time. He hired the thug. That means he likely won't come after us himself but will look for someone else to hire."

True. But if Greg got desperate enough to silence Faith and stop her from remembering that awful night, then he might try to kill them himself.

"I have good security," Theo said, no doubt trying to soothe her.

The second kiss he gave her did some soothing as well. It also gave her another kick of that heat, and she might have leaned in to take a whole lot more from him if his phone hadn't dinged with another call.

He dropped back a step, looked at the screen and said, "Quill." Theo spoke the man's name in the same tone as a really bad curse word.

Kim glanced at Faith and saw that the woman had her eyes closed, so she shut the door so the conversation wouldn't disturb her.

Theo took the call, putting it on speaker.

"Where the hell are you?" Theo demanded.

"Well, I'm not trying to kill you if that's what you're asking," Quill fired back.

"I'm asking where are you. It's a simple question."

"No, it's not, because you want to arrest me for something I didn't do. It's all over town that you think I'm the one who fired those shots at you and your women, and hey, I didn't."

"Prove it," Theo snapped. "Go straight to the sheriff's office and submit to another GSR test."

Quill did some actual cursing. "I can do that, but you've got to swear you won't arrest me. I don't want to be locked up while I'm awaiting trial."

"I'm not promising you anything. You've got a lot of questions to answer, and you need to quit dodging my deputies."

"I'll quit dodging them when they quit trying to arrest me. Hell, Theo, you know I'm not the one trying to kill you."

Kim knew that Theo didn't know that at all. Quill was just as prime of a suspect as Greg and Duran.

"Look, I told you that Rowena's trying to set me up," Quill went on a moment later. "She wants me behind bars, and she'll do anything to make sure that happens."

Again, Kim held her tongue, but she wanted to say the woman didn't have to do anything to put him away for a long time. Well, nothing other than show up in court and testify against him.

"If I didn't know better, I'd think somebody's persuading Rowena to set me up," Quill continued.

And that made Kim think of Greg. Rowena and he had been lovers years ago, but maybe they still had a connection. A connection that would cause Rowena to allow Greg to use her, especially since setting up Quill would benefit the woman by ensuring that he'd end up in jail for a long time.

"You can put all of this in your statement," Theo told the man. "Your suspicions about Rowena, how you feel you've been set up. All of it. Just go to the station now, and I'll arrange for a deputy to start the interview."

Quill certainly didn't jump on that offer. In fact, he cursed again. "I'd think you'd cut me some slack since I'm Jack's grandfather."

"You're a grandparent in name only," Theo was quick to say. "You've never even asked to see Jack."

"Because I knew you'd object." Quill tacked on some profanity to that.

"Yeah, I would have. But a grandparent who cared about his grandson would have at least asked to see him. You didn't. And your shared DNA with my son won't keep you out of a jail cell if you're responsible for what's going on. Trust me on that."

Quill cursed again and ended the call. Theo tried to phone the man right back, but Quill didn't answer. Not a surprise. The man obviously intended to dodge them as long as he could. Kim was hoping, though, that wouldn't be long.

"I'll let Ava know about the call," Theo said as he texted the deputy. "Nothing she can do about it though."

No. But Theo was going after those long shots to locate Quill because he then called the CSIs to see if they could get Quill's location through the phone records. There was little chance Quill would still be there—a definite long shot—but it was worth a try in case he was hunkered down somewhere.

When he finished with the CSIs, he looked up, his gaze connecting with Kim's. He opened his mouth but then closed it and shook his head. "I was about to suggest that you try to grab a nap, like Faith, but I know you won't do that."

Kim made a sound of agreement. She was certainly tired enough to nap, but there was no chance she could turn off her mind. Neither could Theo though he had to be as exhausted as she was.

It was a mistake, of course, but she went to him and pulled him into another hug. She knew what she was doing. Knew that with this supercharged energy between them, it wouldn't stay just a hug.

And she was right.

Almost immediately, Theo's mouth came to hers, and this was no light peck. It was a hard and hungry kiss that was filled with not only the heat but also the emotions of what they'd just been through. It was long, deep and extremely effective at making her want a whole lot more.

Theo clearly wanted more, too, because he backed her against the wall, pressing his body to hers while he took her mouth as if she were the cure for, well, everything. He certainly tasted like the cure to her, too, and she didn't even try to slow him down. Didn't try to tamp down the intensity. She just rode the wave of heat, letting the pleasure crash into her.

Of course, the kissing only led to more need. More fire. And Theo ran his hand between them, cupping her right breast and swiping his thumb over her erect nipple. Kim moaned, trying not to allow any thoughts in her mind that would put a stop to this. She didn't want to stop. She wanted Theo, and she wanted him now.

Theo was on the same page because he fumbled around and opened the door to his bedroom. They didn't stop the kiss or the touching and nearly tumbled into his room when they finally managed to move. Theo got them inside and shut the door.

Kim had just enough common sense left to lock it, as well, in case Faith got up from her nap and walked in on them.

Because she wanted—no, she needed—her hands on him, Kim went after his shirt. It wasn't easy to unbutton it since he obviously wanted her out of her clothes as well. She won that particular battle first and had the victory of being able to run her hands over his bare chest. The man was built. So many muscles, and she got another slam of heat at feeling them respond to her touch.

She responded, too, when Theo shucked off her top, shoved down her bra and lowered his head to kiss her breasts. This time the slam of pleasure made her legs go limp. Theo took care of that though. He just scooped her up and, without stopping the sweet torture of the tongue kisses on her breast, carried her to his bed.

He eased her down on the mattress, following on top of her, and Kim got another pleasure slam by feeling his weight on her. Especially the weight where his sex pressed against hers. That really upped the urgency.

"You'd better have a condom," she managed to say.

Theo didn't answer, not with words anyway. Nor did he stop kissing and touching her. He maneuvered them to the side of the bed and he thankfully took out a condom from his nightstand. She expected him to start shedding the rest of his clothes so he could put it on. But obviously he had other plans.

Really good plans.

Tossing the condom on the mattress beside them, Theo began to trail some slow, wet kisses down her throat. Over her breasts. And to her stomach. He didn't stop there either. Ridding her of her clothes as he went, he kissed each inch of skin that he bared. Kissed and used his clever tongue to skyrocket the heat and pleasure until Kim was ready to beg him to give her release.

Theo didn't release her though. Sliding off her panties, he continued the kissing torture. Continued until Kim was certain she wasn't even capable of begging. She could only lie there and let the wash of pleasure take over. He didn't finish her off that way though. Theo took her right to the brink and then reversed the kisses, sliding his tongue back up her body. By the time he reached her neck, Kim could take no more.

"I want your clothes off now," she demanded.

Theo certainly didn't cooperate with that. He kept kissing, kept touching, kept driving her up, up, up, only to pull back before she could climax.

Cursing him and the hungry gnawing heat, Kim managed to remove his holster and belt. No easy feat. It was an even bigger feat when she shoved down his jeans and boxers.

Oh, yes. The man was built.

Later, she'd take the time to savor his body and return some of the kissing torture he was doling out. For now, though, she just reached for the condom. Theo did help with that, maybe because she began kissing his neck, and that was clearly a hot sexual button for him. He finally hurried. Then slowed again to lock gazes with her when he slipped inside her.

More pleasure came. Man, did it. So much pleasure that she had to fight to stave off the release. Yes, she wanted that. Desperately wanted it, but she wanted to savor this night as much as she could.

His thrusts convinced Kim to quit fighting it. Theo must have realized she was close and that this time he wasn't going to pull back. He simply kissed her, long and deep, and gave her exactly what she needed to fly right over the edge.

Chapter Fifteen

While Theo dried off from his shower, and shower sex, he watched Kim as she dressed. He wanted to see if she was showing any signs of regret for having had sex with him not once but twice.

She wasn't.

Then again, maybe there hadn't been time for regrets to surface. They'd taken a very short reprieve and less than five minutes after they'd both gotten some release from the intense heat, his phone had rung. And it'd continued to ring with reports from Ava to let him know that Quill hadn't been found and that Greg still hadn't showed his face. Maybe that was because he was hiding in fear from Quill, but it was giving Theo a bad feeling.

The bad feeling continued because Duran was doing the opposite of Greg and Quill. He was making himself seen. Maybe too much so by going to his office only to leave ten minutes later to go to a coffee shop for another short stay. Duran could be trying to make himself look innocent by being so visible, but that didn't wash with Theo because he knew the man could have already hired someone else to make another attempt to kill Kim, Faith and him.

"Well, what's the verdict?" Kim asked, drawing his attention back to her. Not that it had strayed far. Kim had a way of occupying his thoughts even when his thoughts should be firmly on the investigation.

He wasn't sure exactly what verdict she meant, so Theo went with the obvious. "Sex with you was great."

That made her smile. For a couple of seconds anyway. "Ditto. I knew it would be and that's why I've avoided you."

Theo understood what she meant. Now that they'd given in to the intense attraction, there was no going back. And that meant they had complications to face. One of those complications surfaced almost immediately when his phone dinged again, and he heaved a sigh.

"Nadia," he relayed to Kim and, like him, she began bracing herself. She also finished dressing.

"Is everything okay?" Theo asked Nadia the moment he answered.

"Yes. I mean there's no sign of a gunman or anything like that, but I wanted you to know that Quill called me."

"Where is he?" Theo couldn't say fast enough.

"He wouldn't tell me. He just went on about how Rowena was setting him up. We both know he's a liar, but he keeps pressing this so much that I have to wonder if it's true. Have you gotten any sense from Rowena that she might be doing something other than what she usually does?"

Theo considered that a moment. Normally, after Quill battered her, Rowena would file charges against him and then try to pull those charges when she either got too afraid of reprisal or if she simply didn't know how to have a life without her abuser. But nothing was "normal" about what had been happening.

"It's possible she is trying to set up Quill," Theo finally admitted. "I'll call her and have another chat."

But there was something about this conversation with Nadia that puzzled him. She sometimes let him know if she had any encounters with her parents, but this felt like, well, more.

"Is there something else you wanted to tell me?" Theo asked.

Nadia certainly didn't jump to assure him there wasn't. She paused a long time and then he heard her sigh. "Look, I know Kim is staying there with you, and I understand why."

Theo silently groaned. He figured Nadia was about to launch into her usual gripes about Kim. But he was wrong.

"I understand why," Nadia repeated. "What I don't understand is why it bothers me so much that you two might get together." She paused again. "It's true, isn't it? You might get together?"

Theo had a nice flash of memories of the great sex with Kim. "Yes," he verified. "Kim and I might get together."

He locked gazes with Kim to see if she would silently dispute that. Nope. But, like him, she did look concerned as to how Nadia would deal with that. Because anything that affected Nadia ultimately affected Jack.

And that's why he wanted to tell Nadia that it

wouldn't be just a fling with Kim. Nadia wouldn't have to worry that Jack would get used to having Kim around only to have her not be around at all. But he didn't have time to say any of that because he got an incoming call from Ava.

"Sorry, but I have to go," Theo told Nadia. "It's a work call."

"All right." A moment later, she repeated that, and he had the feeling that she was trying to apologize for how she'd always reacted to hearing Kim's name. That feeling was enough for now. A start that maybe things could be different in the future.

Of course, nothing could be different until he'd made sure none of them was in danger.

I'll check on Faith, Kim mouthed when he ended the call with Nadia and switched to Ava.

Theo nodded and listened to what Ava had to say. "Rowena stopped by the station. She wants to talk to you."

"Good, because I was about to call her. Put her on," Theo instructed. He heard Ava do that, but he didn't wait for Rowena to say anything. He just went with his gut. "I know you're trying to set Quill up, and I want you to spill everything you've done."

Silence. For a long time. But the woman didn't deny it, which meant his gut was right. "I put the dead rat on my doorstep," Rowena finally admitted. "And I sent him texts to tell him to meet me at places where I knew Kim and you would be, like the hospital. I wanted him to start something with you that would get him tossed back in jail."

He nearly asked how she knew where Kim and he would be, but Theo doubted that was much of a secret. Still, he didn't appreciate the woman giving Quill a sort of road map to their whereabouts.

"You told Quill where we were, and he might have tried to kill us," Theo pointed out to Rowena.

"No." She didn't hesitate that time. "I wouldn't have told him if I'd known there'd be attacks. Do you really believe he could have been the one to shoot at you?"

"Oh, yes. I believe it's possible, and with his history, you should believe it, too."

"No," Rowena insisted. "Quill uses his fists or a knife, not guns."

"And you thought he'd try to use his fists or a knife on Kim or me?" Theo snapped, not bothering to pull back on the anger.

He heard Rowena's sharp sob. "I just thought he'd lose his temper and try to hit you, and then you could arrest him. He shouldn't be out and about. Especially if he gets word about what happened with…well, with me and you know who twenty-one years ago."

Apparently, Rowena was still trying to keep Greg's name under wraps, and Theo couldn't blame her for that. No need to give Quill a reason to go after his battered wife's former lover. But that did give Theo an idea.

"Did Greg ask you to do the things you've done to set Quill up?" Theo prodded.

"Of course not. I haven't talked to him in years, not since we ended things."

Maybe, but Theo would like some proof of that. "Give Deputy Lawson access to your phone records so we can verify you sent those texts to Quill to give him Kim's and my location. It'll also prove you haven't called Greg."

Theo wished he could see the woman's face because he could practically feel the fierce debate she was having with herself. If she refused, he'd just get a warrant and access the phone records, but if she agreed to let Ava have them right away, she might be caught in a lie.

"All right," Rowena finally said. "But I did call Greg earlier. He gave me his number when he was here at the sheriff's office for his interview."

"Mind telling me what you two discussed?" Theo asked.

Again, she hesitated. "I told him to watch out for Quill, that he was a dangerous man."

That was likely the truth, but Theo was betting that wasn't all they'd talked about. "Give Deputy Lawson an account of that conversation. If nothing you two said pertains to the investigation, she'll keep Greg's name to herself."

"Good," Rowena muttered.

When Rowena handed the phone back to Ava, Theo instructed Ava to take a statement about any and all of Rowena's text and phone conversations with Greg and an account of the texts she'd sent Quill in the past forty-eight hours.

He ended the call and made his way into the hall. The guest room door was open, but Kim and Faith weren't there. He heard them in the kitchen and followed the sound of their voices, but what his sister said had him stopping in his tracks for a moment.

"I have to go," Faith said, her voice much stronger than it had been earlier. "I have to see it for myself."

Theo definitely didn't like the sound of that, and it had him moving again. "See what for yourself?" he asked when he walked into the kitchen. Judging from their expressions, Kim and Faith had been involved in a serious debate.

Faith whirled toward him, not with surprise, but she went to him as if searching for an ally. "The house."

No need for him to ask which house. She meant their family home, and Theo looked at Kim to hear her take on this.

Kim dragged in a long breath before she spoke. "When Faith woke up from her nap, she said she remembered something. Not the killer's face," Kim quickly added. "But—"

"But I remember the coat he was wearing," Faith interrupted, her words rushing together. "I remember him carrying me down the stairs and out of the house."

Theo nodded. "All of this is a good start, and I think we should arrange for you to speak with a therapist who might be able to help you recall even more."

Faith shook her head and took hold of his arm. "No. I have to go to the house. I have to see it myself." She stopped, her mouth trembling now. "Because if I see it, I know I'll be able to tell you who killed our parents."

Chapter Sixteen

Kim knew that what Faith had just said had to be a tempting offer for Theo.

I'll be able to tell you who killed our parents.

That had been the question that'd haunted them for twenty-one years. But it just wasn't a safe idea going to the house where that nightmare had happened.

"No," Theo said, looking Faith straight in the eyes. "It's too dangerous for us to go to our old place."

Faith started shaking her head before he'd even finished. "You can make it safe by bringing along a deputy. And I might not even have to get out of the cruiser. I think if I can just see the house, then I'll remember the rest of what I've blocked out."

Judging from Theo's skeptical expression, he wasn't buying that. Neither was Kim. "There are pictures of the place you can look at."

Though that wouldn't be an especially pleasant sight. However, Faith didn't have the same nightmarish memories that Theo and Kim did. They hadn't been able to block out much of anything.

Still shaking her head, Faith turned to her. "No, a picture won't do. I need to be there, to take it all in."

Theo's sigh was long and weary. "Even if we risk a trip like that, there are no guarantees you'll remember any more than you already do."

Faith tapped her finger to her chest. "I can guarantee it. And don't ask me how I know, I just do. Seeing the house will be the trigger that will bring it all back."

Kim couldn't totally dismiss that, but there was still the risk of a killer finding them there.

"Please," Faith added, volleying pleading looks at both of them. Apparently, she didn't get the "let's do it" reaction she wanted because she huffed. "All right, let me borrow one of your deputies, and I'll go without you." She moved closer to Theo to stare at him. "Because one way or another, I am going. We'll finally learn who killed our family and made all of our lives a living hell."

Kim couldn't dispute the "living hell" part either. Yes, Theo and she had healed, some, but it would never be a total healing until they had the answers as to who had set things in motion that night.

"I'll go without you," Faith stated.

Theo just stared at his sister. Or rather, he glared, and maybe he saw the determination or something in Faith's eyes because he cursed. Then he shifted his attention to Kim.

"I don't suppose I could talk you into staying here with a deputy while I go with Faith to the house?" he asked.

Kim didn't even have to think of her response. "No

chance whatsoever of me staying behind. If the two of you go, I go. The three survivors of that night," she tacked on.

Though there was likely one other survivor.

The killer.

Was he monitoring the house to see if they'd go there? Maybe. But it might be the last place he thought they'd ever return. Because of the memories. The flashbacks. The hell it would bring to all of them.

The muscles stirred in Theo's jaw and he took out his phone. Kim wasn't sure who he was calling until she heard him say, "Mike, you've relieved Nelline and are in the cruiser in front of my house?"

Deputy Mike Gonzales. Since Theo put the call on speaker, she heard the deputy answer, "Yes. Something you need, boss?"

"Yeah, I need my head examined," Theo muttered.

"Excuse me?" Mike asked.

Theo didn't repeat that, but he sighed again. "My sister believes she'll recover some of her memories if we go to the house where my parents were murdered."

Mike's silence probably meant he was processing that. "What do you want me to do to make that happen?"

"The four of us will go there in the cruiser," Theo explained. "I'll call the Silver Creek Ranch and see who's available to meet us there. One of my ranch hands will follow up to give us even more backup."

Theo stepped aside to make those calls, but Faith didn't wait. She went to the rack near the door and got the loaner coat that Gage had brought to the hospital with him when he'd done guard duty. Faith peered out

the window, a combination of both nerves and antici-
pation on her face.

"I know this is a risk," she told Kim. "I know I'm
putting both of you in danger, but I need the truth."

All parts of that were true, but Kim sighed and pulled
her into a hug. "We're already all in danger," she reminded Faith, and a part of her wanted to face that danger head-on. To have a final showdown with the killer
who'd taken so much from all of them.

But Theo could be hurt or killed.

That reminder robbed her of her breath and caused
her heart to race. That could happen. Heck, it could happen to all of them, but the same might be true if they
stayed put. They couldn't stay inside Theo's house forever, and the killer had to know that eventually he'd get
another shot at them.

Kim pulled back from the hug and met Faith eye
to eye. "No unnecessary risks. By that I mean, don't
try to bolt from the cruiser. If we get out, Theo has to
agree to it."

She waited for Faith to nod, waited a second longer
to make sure the nod was the truth, and then Kim gave
her own nod before she went to her purse that she'd put
on the highest hook of the rack. She took out her gun
that she'd brought with her and slipped it into the slide
holster in the back of her jeans.

Faith didn't react to the gun as Kim had hoped she
would. She'd thought that Faith might see the weapon
and have it sink in that there could be danger, but judging from her expression, she remained determined to
go to the house.

"Don't do anything to make me regret this," Theo muttered to his sister as he put on his coat.

He, too, waited for Faith to nod. Waited again until Kim gave him the okay. She was really hoping nothing happened for him to regret this either.

"This isn't like when we were kids," she reminded him. "We know how to defend ourselves."

Still, she got a flashback of hiding under the bed with her stuffed bear clutched to her. Maybe Theo saw the effects of that flashback in her eyes because he gave her hand a gentle squeeze before they headed out.

Mike was right there waiting for them with the cruiser already running and warm. Good thing, too, because the temp had dropped, and the wind was whipping across the ranch. It rarely snowed in this part of Texas, but the air felt heavy, cold and wet. Not exactly a good vibe to take with them to the scene of the crime that had changed their lives.

As Mike started the short drive, Theo got another text, and after he responded, he relayed, "Still no sign of Quill." After he said that, he turned and looked at Faith. "Do you remember him?"

She nodded. "Only a little. He worked for Mom and Dad for a while." She paused a moment. "And you were married to his daughter for a couple of years."

"I was. I have a two-year-old son named Jack."

That caused Faith to smile a little. "Maybe when this is over, I can meet him."

Theo made a sound of agreement and looked at her again. "Is it possible Quill was the one who took you that night?"

Faith's smile vanished, and she stayed quiet a moment, obviously considering that. "Maybe." She stopped, repeated it. "He would have known the layout of the house. Would have known where to find me."

Her voice broke on the last word, and Kim figured she was thinking some horrible thoughts right now. That if it hadn't been for her, her parents wouldn't have been killed; that they'd died because someone had wanted to get to her. It wasn't much, but Kim repeated what Theo had done to her earlier by giving Faith's hand a gentle squeeze. Kim didn't even attempt to voice any reassurances that all would be well because she couldn't be certain it would be.

Nothing would be well until they'd caught the killer and made him pay for what he'd done.

With that dismal thought flashing in her head, Kim tried to keep her breath steady when Mike took the turn toward the Sheldon ranch.

Kim hadn't been back to the Sheldon ranch since the night of the murders. In fact, she often went out of her way just so she didn't have to drive by the place. But she actually welcomed seeing it now because, like Faith, she wanted to see if it triggered anything other than the nightmarish memories.

After all, she could have seen the killer, too, and blocked it from her mind. It made her wish that she'd done this trip before. Before there'd been two attempts to kill the three of them.

No one had lived at the place since the murders, and even though she knew Theo often sent in workers to do repairs, the ranch still had that abandoned feeling. No livestock in the pastures, and the barn doors were nailed shut with boards. Maybe to keep out any trespassers.

"When I was reading articles on the Internet, some people called it the murder ranch," Faith muttered.

They did. Kim had seen that on social media. It had also become a place where some teenagers dared each other to go since some believed it to be haunted with the ghosts of the dead.

When Mike drove over a small hill, the house came into view. Even though the sun would set in about a half hour, there was still plenty of light, so Kim could clearly see the place. Once, she'd been thrilled to come here because it meant spending time with her best friend. She certainly wasn't getting any happy feelings now.

She spotted one of the Silver Creek Ranch trucks and saw her uncle Dade behind the wheel. Good. He was a retired deputy and could give them backup if needed.

Dade tipped his head in greeting, but he stayed in the truck. So did the ranch hand who'd followed them there.

"You've been back here since it happened?" Faith asked, aiming the question at Theo.

"When I was eighteen. I thought I was coming to say goodbye to the place because I intended to sell it. Grayson had been managing the upkeep on it, and I figured it was time to let go of it." He paused, his gaze fixed on the two-story white house with what had once been a welcoming porch. "I couldn't sell it. Couldn't burn it to the ground," he added a moment later after he cursed.

Mike pulled to a stop in the curved driveway, positioning the cruiser so it was directly in front of the house. All of them stayed quiet, studying it.

Letting the memories slam into them like sharp knives.

Kim tried not to make any sounds since she knew anything that came out of her mouth right now would be doused in nightmare, but she did meet Theo's eyes for a moment and saw he was feeling the same thing.

Faith moved closer to the window, peering out through the glass. Her gaze swept around the house, the porch, the grounds.

"Yes," Faith muttered. "I remember something."

EVEN THOUGH FAITH had spoken so softly that her words hardly had any sound, Theo still heard her. He snapped toward her and saw that she had her attention pinned to the house.

"What do you remember?" Kim and he asked in unison.

"A silver watch that was blue behind the numbers." Faith kept staring at the house, her eyes fixed as if she were in a trance. "He was wearing one on his left wrist. I was trying to get away from him, but he had me clamped against him as he ran from the house. I saw the watch when he shoved me into a car."

Theo latched onto every one of those details. Not exactly earth-shattering info, not yet anyway, but anything at this point was fresh info that could be used to find the killer.

"Did you see his face?" Kim pressed.

Faith shook her head. "He was wearing a ski mask." She stopped, swallowed hard. "He smelled like blood."

Theo didn't ask her how she recognized that particular smell. Like him, Faith had been raised on a working ranch, and she would have been a witness to some injuries and even some procedures done on the livestock.

"'Blood,'" Kim repeated, and Theo knew what she was thinking. One person working alone could have committed the crimes if he'd done the murders first. Then, he could have easily taken Faith.

And Theo hadn't stopped any of that.

He had to stomp down that thought. That guilt. It would only eat away at him as it'd done for the past twenty-one years, and it sure as heck wouldn't help him keep a clear head. Right now, he needed that and as many little details as Faith could recall so they could try to piece this together.

"What about the car?" Theo asked. "Do you remember anything about it?"

Faith stayed quiet a moment. "It had four doors because he opened the back and tossed me on the seat. Then he jammed a needle in my leg. It hurt, and I yelled. Maybe I yelled," she amended. She shook her head. "He shoved something in my mouth. A wad of gauze, I think."

It twisted at him to hear what Faith had been put through that night. Dragged from her home, drugged and kidnapped. So many things could have gone wrong, and she could have ended up dead.

"I woke up in a bed," Faith continued. "But I was woozy, and the man in the ski mask kept giving me shots." She paused again, probably because she had to. Her breathing was so fast that talking had to be hard. Especially talking about all of this. "I don't know how long that went on."

And when the drugging had finally ended, the Neelys had lied and told her she'd been in an accident. They'd brainwashed her into believing she was their daughter.

"Other than the blood, ski mask, watch, and the car, do you remember anything else about the man?" Kim asked. "His scent? His size?" she prompted when Faith didn't respond.

After several long moments, Faith shook her head and made a sound of frustration. "Let me keep thinking."

Theo gave her that time, but he sent a quick text to Ava.

If Rowena's still with you, ask her if Quill ever owned a silver watch with a blue face.

It didn't take Ava long to answer.

Rowena says he's owned a lot of watches, that he buys a new one every year or so, and that one of them might have been silver and blue.

Hell. A *might* wasn't going to cut it. He needed proof.

Get a search warrant for Quill's house, Theo instructed. Go through all his watches and see if there's a silver and blue one.

Of course, the odds were slim that Quill had kept it all this time, but if he had, there could still be traces of blood on it. That was exactly the kind of link that Theo had been searching for.

"I need to go inside," Faith insisted. "I need to see where I was taken from."

Theo didn't even have to consider this. "No. You're not getting out of the cruiser."

Faith whirled around to face him, no doubt ready to argue, when the ground around them exploded into a fireball.

Chapter Seventeen

Kim heard the blast a split second before the cruiser went flying. Her brain didn't register what was happening at first, not until the vehicle landed with a hard thud. Around them, there were other deafening blasts, and that's when she realized that someone was trying to kill them.

"Explosives," Theo shouted, and Kim could see him trying to assess their situation.

Their situation definitely wasn't good.

There was a massive hole to the right of the cruiser and another in front between it and Dade's truck. Both the truck and Dade seemed to be fine, but the front end of the cruiser was a tangled mess. The blast had torn it apart and there was steam spewing from the busted radiator.

Kim looked behind her at Theo's ranch hand. The front of his truck had been blown to smithereens, as well, and the windshield was cracked and webbed, but she could see some movement behind the glass and prayed that he hadn't been hurt.

"Someone set bombs?" Faith blurted.

Faith was fighting to get out of her seat belt, no doubt so she could go into a panicked run, but Kim held on to her even though she wasn't sure how long they could stay put. She especially wasn't sure of that when there was another blast that jolted through the cruiser, tossing them around like ragdolls. Kim was certain if they all hadn't still been wearing their seat belts, they would have been seriously injured.

Or worse.

Theo cursed, and Kim followed his gaze as it slashed to the front of the cruiser. Except there wasn't much left for them to see. And then Kim caught a scent she didn't want to smell.

Gasoline.

Both Mike and Theo cursed again. "We have to get out now," Theo insisted. "There's enough of the engine left that the gas could cause it to blow."

That could burn them alive, and this time when Faith started to release her belt, Kim didn't stop her. Kim undid her own seat belt and drew her weapon, getting ready for what could be an attempt to gun them down. The killer could have set the explosives, hoping that would kill them, but since they hadn't, he could be out there waiting for them.

Theo threw open his door and looked back at his ranch hand. "Carver, are you okay?"

Carver Daniels, a man who'd worked for Theo for years. "I'm not hurt," he answered right away. "I think we need to get out of here though."

"Agreed," Theo barked and then called out, "Dade, we're heading to your truck." He'd probably chosen that one because it had the least amount of damage and was already parked facing the road for a faster exit. "Faith and Kim will go inside with you. The rest of us will get in the truck bed. The second we're in, take off."

Kim didn't like that plan one bit. She knew they wouldn't all fit inside the cab of the truck, but she didn't care for the fact that Theo would be in the bed where he'd be an easy target for a sniper. Still, there wasn't time to argue. She could only hope and pray that all of them would make it out of there alive.

"Move now," Theo told them.

They did, but Kim had barely made it a step when there was another explosion, and her heart dropped to her stomach when she saw the front of Dade's truck go up in flames. Dade had to bolt from his vehicle.

"Take cover," Theo yelled.

Dade hurried back to them, taking hold of Faith's arm to get her moving to a thick cluster of pecan trees. The rest of them followed, all dropping down so they wouldn't be easy targets.

"We could go inside the house," Faith muttered, her voice shaking like the rest of her.

"It could be rigged with explosives, too," Theo fired back.

Yes, it could be. In fact, maybe that's what the killer wanted, all of them inside the house so he could finish what he'd started twenty-one years ago.

The flashbacks came like fists, slamming into Kim, robbing her of her breath and causing the panic to rise in her throat. She heard the strangled sound she made and hated it. Because it alerted Theo, and he scurried toward her. He put his left arm around her, pulling her to him. Not good. She needed him to focus on their surroundings and not her.

"I'm all right," she said. At the moment, it was a huge lie. She wasn't all right by any means, but she soon would be. Kim had no intention of letting the fear and the flashbacks get them killed.

"The killer wouldn't want us in the house," Kim murmured more to herself than Theo. "That could trigger us remembering something about him. Something that would tell us who he is."

Theo made a quick sound of agreement just as there was another explosion. Not in or near the house but rather by the vehicles again. The blast shook the ground beneath them and ripped apart even more of the cruiser.

Obviously, someone had set explosives there in the driveway, figuring that, eventually, they would return. Or rather, Faith would. Whoever had put the explosives in place had to be watching them.

Waiting for them.

Kim got confirmation of that a split second later when the first shot came bashing into one of the trees.

HELL. THEO DEFINITELY hadn't wanted to deal with a gunman when there were explosives tearing up the vehicles. Worse, there could be explosives waiting to rip apart the ground beneath them.

But he rethought that.

If there were bombs in the trees, the killer would have set them off when they'd run for cover. So the shots were likely meant to draw them out, to get them running so they could be picked off. Or rather, so Kim, Faith and he could be killed. Theo was pretty sure that the killer would consider Dade and Carver collateral damage.

A bullet slammed into the pecan tree right next to Faith. Way too close. Theo took hold of her arm and pulled her deeper into the grove. Thankfully, there were a lot of trees, nearly two dozen, that were already tall and mature when his parents were still alive. There was now enough thick undergrowth beneath them that, hopefully, would give them some good places to hole up until...

Well, until he could put a stop to this.

And he would have to stop the shooter. No way did he want any more of his deputies or the Rylands running into this danger. He needed to pinpoint the shooter and try to get to him. First, though, he had to make sure Kim and Faith were safe.

"This way," Theo instructed Kim and Carver in a whisper as he continued to lead Faith toward the center of the grove.

Moving them there was somewhat of a risk since the killer could have hired someone to lay in wait for them. However, staying near the line of fire wouldn't be smart either.

Once he reached some thick shrubs, he motioned for Faith and Kim to get down. "Wait here," he added.

But Kim took hold of his left hand. "You're not going out there," she insisted. Even in the thick part of the grove, there was still plenty of light for him to see the fear in her eyes. Not fear for herself, he knew, but for him.

Theo considered trying to reassure her that he would

be all right, but this was Kim, and she would know he
had no way of guaranteeing that. He wished he could.
Not just so he could erase that look in her eyes but because he truly wanted to put an end to the danger so he
could tell her how much she meant to him. How much
he wanted her in his life.

"Don't you dare get hurt or killed," Kim said before
he could figure out what to say.

For some reason, that made him smile. It was very
short-lived thanks to another round of gunfire, but Theo
still took a second to brush a kiss on her mouth.

"No getting hurt or killed," he murmured, and then
he looked at Faith. "Stay down and stay put," he added
in a warning.

He could see his sister's eyes, too, and she was worried as well. She also looked fed up with being the target
of someone who'd already ruined her life by kidnapping
her. Faith looked ready to do something foolish, like
make herself a target to draw out this SOB, and that's
why Theo repeated his warning. Whether or not she'd
obey, he didn't know, and that's why he had to hurry.

"Make sure the killer doesn't get to them," Theo
told Carver.

He knew he could trust his ranch hand to do whatever was needed to keep Kim and his sister safe, but
it was still hard leaving them there and walking away.

Theo went back toward the front of the grove where
Dade was positioned behind one of the larger trees.
Since Dade was a retired deputy, he had plenty of experience in dangerous situations, and, like Carver, Theo
knew he could trust Dade to help in any way he could.

Right now, Theo needed him to make sure a gunman didn't come charging in to get to Faith and Kim.

"The shots are coming from that direction," Dade pointed out, tipping his head to the west. Specifically, to the area by the barn.

Dade had taken aim there but hadn't fired, maybe because he wasn't sure if Theo had workers on the grounds. He didn't. And that's why Theo lifted his gun and looked around. He didn't see anyone, and the barn doors were boarded up, but it was possible the gunman had knocked a hole in the wood and was firing from there. It was also possible, though, that the guy was either on the roof or in the hayloft.

"Let me see if I can get him to show himself," Theo muttered, and he sent two bullets into the wall to the right of the barn door.

The gunman responded and responded fast. Not by showing himself but by sending two rounds of fire in Theo's direction. Like Dade, Theo had already taken cover, had been expecting the retaliation, but the angle of the shots gave him some critical info.

"He's on the roof," Theo relayed to Dade.

Theo hadn't left any ladders around to tempt trespassers into using it to gain access to the second floor of the house where the windows weren't boarded up, but the shooter could have brought a ladder with him. If so, he would have needed a vehicle and had probably parked either behind the house or along one of the ranch trails.

"I've got plenty of ammo," Dade told him. "You want

us to double team and just start shooting at the roof? We might get lucky."

Yeah, they might, but since there was no telling how long the guy had been there waiting for them, he'd likely set up in the position where he was least likely to be shot. After all, the SOB would have known that Theo would return fire. Besides, it could be the shooter who got lucky and managed to hit and kill one of them. Maybe even Faith or Kim. Depending on the weapon the guy was using, none of them was out of range of the shots.

And that meant Theo had to stop and catch this snake.

It wouldn't do for the gunman to keep firing until he ran out of ammo because then he would just flee. No doubt using that ladder he'd brought with him. Then he could regroup and come after them again.

Theo wanted to end this right here, right now.

Twenty-one years was too damn long to wait for justice. Added to that, neither Kim nor Faith would be safe as long as this killer was still out there.

"I'm going to circle around," Theo told Dade, "and come up from behind him."

Dade immediately glanced around, assessing if that was even possible. It was. Even though this place was no longer home for him, Theo knew it like the back of his hand.

"I can cut through these pecan trees to that row of mountain laurels," Theo explained just as more shots came their way.

The mountain laurels wouldn't provide as much protection as the trees, but they might give him enough cover so he wouldn't be seen. He could follow them all the way to the back of the house and use the shrubs on the other side to get to the barn.

"You keep him busy by firing shots at him," Theo told Dade. "I'll text you when I'm close to the barn so you won't hit me with friendly fire."

Dade made a quick sound of agreement. "You should go ahead and let Carver know you'll be moving around. Don't want him to mistake you for the gunman."

"Good point," Theo muttered, and he took care of that right away.

The moment Theo started moving, Dade fired a shot at the barn roof. Theo knew that Dade wouldn't make the diversion obvious. Instead, Dade paced his fire and, judging from the sound of the shots, wasn't aiming at the same spot each time. He was spreading the bullets around, and Theo could hope Dade would get lucky and hit the guy.

Threading his way around the pecan trees, Theo moved fast and tried not to think about Kim and his sister. Tried and failed. He was worried for their safety. Worried that he'd fail again as he had the night his parents had been killed. It ate away at him to think of losing Faith.

Of losing Kim.

Mercy, he wouldn't lose her. Not when they'd finally managed to break down some old barriers so they actually stood a chance of being together.

Because of where he'd positioned Kim, Faith and Carver, Theo couldn't see them, and he forced his mind off them so he wouldn't miss anything that might end up getting them all killed. After all, the shooter on the roof might be just another hired gun, and the killer could be waiting for his chance to go after them.

Theo had just made it to the mountain laurels when he heard something he didn't want to hear. Faith.

"I remember who you are," his sister shouted.

Hell. What was she doing? The gunman could use the sound of her voice to identify her position.

"It won't do you any good to kill us because I just sent off a text to everyone I know, telling them who you are," Faith shouted. "I remember the watch, your boots, the car you used. I remember the smell of blood on your clothes, but most of all, I know who you are."

It was a bluff.

Well, probably.

If Faith had truly recalled the name of the person who'd killed their parents and kidnapped her, she would have used the name. His sister was obviously trying to save them by taking away the killer's motive to murder them.

"I know who you are," Faith repeated, and Theo could hear some kind of struggle going on. Probably because Carver and Kim were trying to hush Faith and keep her down so she wouldn't be shot. After all, if Theo figured it was a bluff, then the killer would as well.

Cursing, Theo knew he had to change his plans. He sent quick texts to Carver and Dade to let them know he'd be approaching the area where he'd left Kim and his sister, but Theo hadn't had time to head that direction when he heard another sound.

Someone screamed.

Chapter Eighteen

Kim wasn't sure how things had turned so ugly so fast, but they had. And if she didn't do something right away, they could get even worse.

One second, Faith had been muttering to herself that she had to do something to save them, and the next the woman had jumped up from the ground and started shouting. She might as well have put a big neon sign on herself to advertise to the killer where he could shoot her.

"Get down and stay quiet," Kim whispered to Faith, and she tried to wrestle her back to the ground.

Faith didn't cooperate with that one bit. She continued to yell and, as Kim had suspected, the gunman started sending bullets their way. Thankfully, there were enough trees between them and the shooter that the shots were slamming into the thick trunks. But that might not last. If the killer could chip away enough of the wood, then he might be able to put them in his sights.

Carver joined in the wrestling match to pull Faith down, and they'd just managed to get her back to the ground when Kim heard Carver's phone ding.

"It's Theo," the hand relayed once he'd had a chance to see the text. "He's heading our way."

Kim wanted to curse because, if Theo was moving, it meant he wasn't taking cover, something they all needed to be doing right now.

"Don't put your brother in danger by trying to get back up," Kim warned Faith.

That warning finally seemed to get through. Faith wasn't saving them by taunting the killer. Instead, she was leading the guy straight to them.

Kim's head came up when she heard a rustling sound to her right. Someone was moving through the trees, trampling down the thick underbrush. She was certain it was Theo.

But she was wrong.

Both Carver and she whipped their guns in the direction of those footsteps when the man bolted through the trees and into a small clearing in front of them. Definitely not Theo.

Greg.

"Put your hands in the air," Kim demanded, and she moved away from Faith so she could shoot Greg if necessary.

However, Greg wasn't armed. Or rather, he didn't have a gun in either of his hands. Kim could see that when he lifted them in the air as she'd ordered. But he was wearing a bulky coat with plenty enough room to hide a small arsenal.

"Faith," Greg said, the single word rushing out with his gusting breath. "Are you all right?"

Kim wasn't sure what to make of the man calling

her Faith instead of Ashley. Or what to make of Greg's concern. Probably an act. If so, he could be playing the worried ex-boyfriend so he could get close enough to kill them.

But she had to rethink that, too.

Rethink it because the gunman continued to fire and one of the bullets slammed into a tree a fraction from Greg's head. The man automatically dropped to the ground and cursed.

"We have to get Faith out of here," Greg insisted.

Kim wanted to roll her eyes. "Someone's trying to kill us. We're pinned down. How did you know we were here?"

"I followed you," Greg readily admitted. "I needed to see Faith, to tell her I want her back."

Despite the deafening shots continuing to tear into the trees, Faith made a sound of raw outrage. "Are you the one who kidnapped me?" she snarled.

Even though he was on his belly now, Greg lifted his head enough to look at her. "No." With his eyes wide, he repeated it. "You know it wasn't me. I heard you. You said you remembered who it was, and if you remembered, you know I didn't do that. I'm certainly not the one firing the shots since I'm right here in front of you."

"Then who is shooting?" Kim snapped before Faith could say anything.

Still looking confused, or maybe pretending to be, Greg shook his head. "I don't know."

Kim was about to demand more, but the sound of footsteps stopped her. "Keep your gun on Greg," she instructed Carver, and Kim turned her weapon in the direction of the sound.

This time, though, it was Theo.

Kim felt the slam of both relief and fear. Relief because he appeared to be unharmed, but he was also on his feet and an easy target. His gaze swept around, taking in the situation, and while turning his gun toward Greg, Theo scrambled to Faith and her.

Of course, Theo didn't pull Kim into his arms, but he moved close enough to her so they were shoulder to shoulder, and that helped steady her nerves some. Then again, just having him there had already started the steadying.

"Why is he here?" Theo asked, tipping his head to Greg.

"I needed to make sure Faith was all right." Greg spoke up. "I know you don't believe me, you think that I only want to be with her because of her money, but I really do love her."

Theo huffed. "Cover me while I frisk him," he told Kim and Carver.

He stayed low, crouching, while he made his way to Greg. And with all the efficiency of a veteran cop, he had Greg patted down within seconds. Theo yanked a small handgun from the back waist of the man's jeans and shoved it in his own coat pocket.

Since the shots were continuing nonstop, Theo latched onto the back of Greg's coat and dragged him closer to one of the trees. Not near Faith and Kim though. Theo obviously wanted to keep some space between them.

"Who's shooting at us?" Theo demanded. "Someone you hired? Or is it Duran?"

Again, Greg acted surprised. "I have no idea who's shooting. Faith said she knew."

Faith opened her mouth and Kim was certain the woman was about to own up to her lie about knowing the identity of the killer. Kim didn't want her to do that, and she figured Theo didn't either. Best to let Greg believe they knew so he could maybe spill something that would tell them who the killer was. Then again, it could indeed be Greg. That's why Kim kept her gun aimed at him.

Even over the gunfire, Kim heard more rustling, and her gaze slashed to Theo's. "Is that Uncle Dade?" she asked.

He immediately shook his head. "Dade would have texted me to let me know he was approaching."

Oh, mercy. Then it could be the killer. He could be using a hired gun to keep them pinned down so he could get closer. If so, he wasn't exactly being silent about his approach. He was trampling through the dead leaves and twigs.

Theo put his index finger to his mouth in a stay-quiet gesture, and he pivoted in the direction of the noise. Since Carver kept his gun trained on Greg, Kim adjusted enough so she, too, would be able to shoot whoever was coming at them now.

But the person stopped.

So did the other gunfire.

And for several heart-stopping moments, there was

just the silence. The only sounds were their gusting breaths and the winter wind in the trees.

Then all hell broke loose.

Someone, a woman, made a feral shout and came bursting through the underbrush.

Rowena.

She had a gun, and she started firing.

OF ALL THE people Theo had considered might start shooting at them, Rowena hadn't been on his list. In fact, he'd never seen the woman show any signs of aggression. Just the opposite. She'd kowtowed to Quill for decades.

But she sure as hell wasn't kowtowing now.

Theo dived away from her, tossing himself in front of Kim and Faith so they wouldn't be hit. However, Rowena wasn't even trying to shoot at them. No. She appeared to be trying to kill Greg, though the woman's shots were going wild and missing everything but some trees.

"Stop," Theo shouted to her.

He stayed down, but he could now hear the woman sobbing. Maybe it was because of the crying that she hadn't been able to aim well. It was also possible, though, that she simply didn't know how to hit a target.

"Rowena," Greg yelled and, with his hands covering his head, tried to scramble away from her. "Why are you doing this?"

Theo wanted to know the same damn thing, but first he needed to stop Rowena from firing again. Since she didn't seem to be listening to demands for her to cease fire, Theo launched himself at her and tackled her. It was a risk, anything he did at this point would be, but he had to take that gun from her.

Rowena didn't make the disarming easy. She fought to get away from Theo, all the while trying to take aim at Greg.

"He has to pay for what he did," Rowena rasped. "Greg has to pay."

"I agree, if he's done something wrong," Theo told her while they struggled. He finally managed to knock the gun from her hand, and Carver moved in to scoop it up from the ground before she could try to grab it again.

Rowena made another of those feral sounds of protest, but the fight finally seemed to go out of her. Her body went limp beneath Theo, and she began to sob even louder.

"She's lost her mind," Greg insisted. His voice was shaking. He probably was, too, but Theo didn't look in his direction yet. He focused on Rowena.

Theo whispered the woman's name, hoping that if he stayed calm—well, as calm as he could be considering what had just happened—that she'd stop crying long enough for him to find out what the heck was going on. First, though, he needed to alert Carver to a possible problem.

"Since the gunman stopped firing, it means the guy could be on the move," Theo explained. "Everyone needs to keep watch. Kim send a text to Dade to let him know what's going on."

With that taken care of, Theo maneuvered himself off Rowena, and rolled the woman onto her back so he could face her. "Now, tell me what it is that you believe Greg's done."

She shook her head from side to side and pressed her hand to her mouth for a moment. "He used me so he could get to Faith. He's the one who took her."

"I did not," Greg practically shouted.

"He did," Rowena insisted. "I put it all together, and I went back through the conversations we had. He asked me about Faith."

Well now, that was interesting, especially considering Greg shouldn't have even known Ashley and his sister were the same person. Faith must have thought so, as well, because she gasped. This had to be a shock for her, too, especially considering she had once intended to marry the man.

"What specifically did Greg ask about Faith?" Theo asked Rowena.

"I just wanted to know who she was," Greg blurted out before Rowena could speak. "I saw her in town, and she looked so much like the daughter the Neelys had lost. I thought maybe she was a relative."

Theo fired one short glare at Greg. "And you asked Rowena about her because you were planning on kidnapping Faith to give her to your good friends."

"No," Greg snapped just as Rowena said, "Yes. He asked me a lot of questions about her, including where she lived."

That put some ice in Theo's blood, and his glare got a whole lot worse. "I'll ask this once, and you'd sure as hell better not lie. Did you kill my parents and kidnap Faith?"

"No." Greg's answer was fast and adamant. Theo still wasn't convinced, and he wished he had Greg in an interview room so he could grill him. This wasn't the time or the place to do a thorough interrogation. "I've told you I had nothing to do with any of that." He paused and made a sob that sounded similar to the ones Rowena was making. "But I think I know who did."

Slowly, and while he tried to rein in the fury slamming through him, Theo turned to Greg.

"Then, tell me now." Theo spoke each word through clenched teeth and a boatload of fury. If this SOB had known all this time who'd committed those god-awful crimes, then Greg was going to pay for keeping his silence.

"You did this to me?" Faith yelled, interrupting whatever Greg had been about to say. Or what he'd been about to lie about anyway.

Faith didn't wait, though, for Greg to respond, and his sister must have believed he was indeed the man who'd taken her that night because she launched herself at him. She tackled Greg much as Theo had done to Rowena, but Faith didn't stop there. She began to punch and kick the man.

Theo had to move away from Rowena to get to Faith. He doubted she could actually kill Greg with her bare hands, but Theo didn't want Greg to be able to file any charges for not protecting him.

It wasn't easy, not with Faith fighting as if her life depended on it, but Theo finally managed to grab a handful of her coat and haul her off the guy. Greg was whimpering now like a wounded animal, but Theo couldn't see anything on his face beyond a few scrapes and red marks.

"He needs to die," Faith yelled, still fighting Theo. "He killed our parents, and he needs to die."

"If Greg did that, he'll be punished," Theo assured her. He took hold of Faith's shoulder to force eye contact and repeated what he'd just said.

"If?" Faith howled. "You heard what Rowena told you."

"And Rowena might be wrong," Theo said, keeping his voice low and with just a tinge of a warning in case Faith was thinking about trying to have another go at Greg.

"I'm not wrong," Rowena said through her sobs, but she quickly amended that. "I don't think I'm wrong."

There it was. That shadow of doubt that would get Greg a not-guilty verdict if this ever went to trial. They were a long way from anything like a trial though. First, they had to get the heck out of there.

Theo glanced around to assess the best route for them to use, but a sound stopped him. Not gunfire or a scream this time. It was more of a muffled gasp, followed by the sounds of frantic movement. He turned.

And his heart dropped to the ground.

Because he saw a man in a ski mask dragging Kim away.

KIM HEARD THE footsteps behind her.

A millisecond too late.

Before she could even turn around to see who it was, someone knocked her gun from her hand and grabbed her by the hair, yanking it so hard that she could have sworn she saw stars. The person—a man—dragged her to a standing position with her back against his chest, and he started moving.

Fast.

So fast that Kim barely got a glimpse of Theo when he realized what was happening. And what was happening was that someone was trying to kidnap her. She had no doubts—none—that the someone was the killer.

The fear slammed through her, but Kim tried not to let it immobilize her. She had to fight. To think. She had to figure out a way to stop herself from being murdered.

At the moment, her abductor obviously didn't want her dead or he could have just killed her when he was sneaking up on her. That meant he probably needed her as a shield so he could escape, or else he wanted her as a bargaining tool. Maybe to draw out Theo and Faith so he could kill all three of them.

But who was doing this?

Who had her in a chokehold and was dragging her through the trees and underbrush?

It wasn't Greg. Kim had been keeping an eye on the man since he'd showed up. She'd watched Rowena, as well, and the woman hadn't moved after Faith had gone after Greg. So was this Quill or Duran?

Maybe.

But it could be just another hired gun, a thug, who was dragging her toward the real killer.

Kim got another slam of fear when she heard Theo call out for her. The sound of running footsteps followed, and she had no doubts that Theo was coming after her. And that would make him an easy target. It didn't take long for that to happen. Her captor stopped right by the last pecan tree in the cluster and, with her in front of him, ducked behind the tree for cover.

He fired a shot at Theo.

"Get down," Kim yelled. But she knew her warning had come too late.

She was almost too afraid to look, but when she did, she finally saw that Theo had dived to the ground, hopefully out of the line of fire.

"There are nearly a dozen lawmen and retired cops heading this way," Theo called out. "And there's no way in hell I'm letting you escape with Kim."

There was so much anger and determination in Theo's voice. Kim wanted to hold on to it, to let it assure her that they'd all get out of this alive, but there were no guarantees. Maybe no second chances, and it crushed her heart to know she might die without ever telling Theo how she felt about him.

That she was in love with him.

It was something she should have told him after they'd had sex. She'd certainly known her feelings then. But now it could be too late for him to ever know.

Her captor fired another shot and Kim prayed it had missed Theo. She had no way of knowing, though, because the guy started moving again. This time, he darted across the small clearing toward the road. It was possible he had a vehicle there waiting, and if so, he could be taking her somewhere to use her as bait.

Bait that would work.

Because Theo would come after her. She had no doubt

about that, and Kim was betting the killer knew that as well. In fact, he'd be counting on it.

Kim felt herself falling and then she landed hard in the deep ditch by the road. The fall didn't loosen the man's grip on her, though, and she didn't have enough of a footing yet to try to kick him. So she tried something else. A ploy that might distract him enough that he wouldn't be able to get a clean shot when Theo came barreling after them.

"Faith remembered who you are," Kim said.

She didn't whisper it, didn't make it sound like a ploy or question. She wanted him to believe that he'd just been outed. It was a long shot. But it worked. She heard the man curse and instantly recognized his voice.

Quill.

There was no mistaking it since she'd heard one of his profanity-laden tirades often enough.

"Then everybody who heard Faith will have to die," Quill concluded.

Kim's mind was reeling with the slam of adrenaline and the fear for Theo, but she forced herself to think of something, anything, that might make Quill back off. "Rowena was there. She heard. Are you going to try to kill her, too?"

That brought on more profanity. "Damn right, I will. She should have died a long time ago."

"Twenty-one years ago." Kim threw it out there. She purposely raised her voice so that Theo could hear her. Not only because he could pinpoint their location in the ditch but also because she wanted him to hear if Quill was about to confess. "Did Rowena help you kill Theo's parents and kidnap Faith?"

"No. Hell, no," Quill snapped. "She's not smart enough for that, and she has no spine."

"Rowena couldn't have killed two people," Kim added, and she had to fight another slam. Not adrenaline this time but pure raw anger. This SOB had murdered two wonderful people and made life a living hell for Theo, Faith and her.

"No, she couldn't have," Quill agreed, as if that were a weakness.

"But you did," Kim continued.

"Yeah, because I had to. They were supposed to be asleep, and they caught me sneaking in. I didn't have a choice."

Oh, yes. He'd had plenty of choices that night, but Quill had made the worst one. "Did Duran pay you to kidnap Faith or was it Greg?"

"Neither. It was the Neelys. Greg told him about this girl he'd seen in Silver Creek. A girl the spitting image of their dead kid. Greg put them in touch with me, and they paid me a hundred thousand to get the kid."

Kim hoped the Neelys had been gut-punched when they'd heard Quill had killed two people to get Faith. But maybe not. Maybe they'd just been so pleased about getting a daughter that they hadn't cared. It was too bad they were both dead or they could have been arrested for the part they had played in this nightmare.

Even though Quill still had his arm anchored around her neck, Kim managed to move her feet, and she found solid ground. Good thing, too, since she heard the movement to her right and she knew that couldn't be good. It was either Theo, who could be gunned down, or a thug Quill had hired.

"The Neelys paid you a hundred grand," Kim repeated. "And when Faith started to remember, you hired a gunman to try to kill her. Or maybe you were the shooter at the hospital."

"I was," Quill answered almost absently, but his body tensed. He was bracing for a fight. "Now shut up so I can hear if your boyfriend's trying to sneak up on us. I've got to finish this."

Finish this. By adding yet more killings to his list of crimes.

"You must have gotten awfully nervous when Nadia hooked up with Theo," Kim went on, hoping that her voice would cover the sound if Theo was indeed sneaking up on them.

"Yeah, you could say that." Quill gave a dry laugh. "I knew Theo was still poking around in the investigation, but then I figured it was a good thing he was with Nadia, that if he said something she'd mention it to Rowena, and Rowena would whine about it to me."

Too bad that hadn't happened, but the investigation hadn't pointed to Quill until after these latest attacks.

"You sent me those letters," Kim insisted. "Why? Why not just stay quiet and let your crimes stay buried?"

"The letters," he repeated like profanity. "Those were a mistake. But I figured if you thought Faith was alive and that her kidnapper, or she, was taunting you, that you wouldn't be looking close to home for the person responsible. I figured you definitely wouldn't be looking right under your own nose."

So, the letters had been an attempt to throw Theo and her off his scent. And in a way, they had worked because it had muddied the waters of the investigation.

"I kept tabs on Faith," Quill went on. "And after the Neelys died, I heard she was snooping around, looking into the Sheldons' missing kid and their deaths. I knew that couldn't be good, and I had to do something to stop her."

Quill's solution to stopping Faith had obviously been to kill them all. New murders to cover up old murders and a kidnapping.

"Sheriff, if you want to keep your woman alive, you'll need to do as I say," Quill called out.

"I'm listening," Theo assured him a moment later.

"Good. Call off your deputies and all those badge-carrying Rylands. This is between you and me. I'll trade Kim for you. All you have to do is surrender."

Oh, mercy. No. Kim didn't want Theo to even consider that. But Theo had to know that Quill intended to murder them all, so he wouldn't just go in without a way to save himself and her.

"All right," Theo agreed. "First, though, tell me if you're the one who set the explosives and if there are any more."

"Of course, I set them," Quill readily admitted. "I've got a militia buddy who taught me how, and I reckoned that sooner or later, you'd be bringing your sister back here. If not, then I would have figured out another way to get to her."

"And what about hired guns?" Theo pressed. "We've got the dead one, but is there another?"

Kim could tell Theo had moved his position and was closer now. It was possible he'd already arranged for Dade or Carver to circle around and come up on Quill from behind. They wouldn't have clean shots because she would be in the way, which meant Kim had to do something.

She adjusted her feet again, intending to drop her weight so that someone would have a head shot for Quill. However, before Kim could do that, she heard someone she didn't want to hear.

"Quill," someone yelled.

Faith.

And Kim just knew the running footsteps she heard was Faith charging toward them. She'd probably heard Quill confess to murdering her parents and kidnapping her, and judging from the sound of her voice, Faith was in a state of pure rage. Rage that could get her killed.

Kim went ahead and dropped down, but she also rammed her elbow into Quill's gut. The man grunted and cursed her. What he didn't do was loosen his grip. He managed to hang on to her.

"Faith, no!" Theo shouted.

From the corner of her eye, Kim saw Faith launch herself at Quill, and she rammed into them, sending all three of them to the ground. Kim didn't try to move away. Instead, she located Quill's right hand and latched onto it, clawing her fingernails into his wrist.

Quill howled in pain and backhanded her, the impact hitting her right in the jaw. This time, she had no choice but to stagger back, but she didn't break the hold she had on his shooting hand.

Even though she couldn't see Theo, Kim knew when he'd reached them. He dropped down into the ditch, maneuvering his body so that he was between Quill and her. Theo made Quill pay by bashing his head with his gun. Quill staggered back just a fraction, and Theo punched Quill in the gut.

Theo probably hadn't wanted to risk firing a shot, not with Faith and her right there, but the punch was effective enough. Quill finally released his grip on the gun, no doubt so he could shove his fist into Theo's face. The man was still going to try to fight his way out of this.

But the gunshot stopped him.

The sound tore through Kim's ears and sent a stab of pain across her entire head. For a moment, she thought she'd been shot, but it was just the reverberation of the bullet being fired.

A shot that could have hit Theo.

That gave Kim a jolt of terror and she got images even worse than the ones she'd been battling for twenty-one years. Her heart stopped, her breath stalled in her chest, everything inside pinpointed to Theo. He had to be all right. He just had to be. She couldn't lose him now.

Theo looked at her, and he seemed to be experiencing his own moment of terror. There were spatters of blood on his face, but Kim couldn't see an actual wound.

Not until she looked at Quill.

He had no color in his face, not a drop. But, mercy, there was plenty of blood. It was on his chin and chest, and he clamped his hands over the gaping, bleeding wound in his chest. His dull, dying eyes went not to Theo or her.

But to Faith.

Faith was holding a gun that Kim recognized because it belonged to her. Quill had knocked it from her hand when he'd dragged her out from that pecan grove.

"I picked it up," Faith said, glancing down at the gun that she kept pointed at Quill. She wasn't shaking, didn't appear to be in shock. In fact, Faith looked steady and resolved that she'd finally gotten justice for her parents and herself.

Still clutching his chest, Quill dropped to his knees. "You killed me," he gurgled out, his gaze fixed on Faith.

"Yes," Faith admitted. "Payback's a bitch, isn't it?"

Quill managed a sneer before the last breath he'd ever take rattled in his throat. He collapsed onto the frozen ground.

Theo waited a moment and then pressed his fingers to Quill's throat. "Dead," he relayed.

There was no relief in his eyes though. No hint of satisfaction that the man who'd murdered his parents was dead. "Get down in the ditch," Theo told them. "I'm not sure if Quill was the one firing shots at us from the barn. There could be a gunman about to carry out Quill's orders to kill us."

Chapter Nineteen

Theo hated the stark fear that shot through Kim's and his sister's eyes. With Quill dead, they'd no doubt thought the danger was over.

But there could be another round.

Theo wasn't even sure there was a gunman out there, but according to the text he'd just gotten, Dade was looking for the guy. So were Grayson, Gage, Kade, Nate and Mason, who'd arrived at the ranch shortly after Quill had managed to grab Kim. If there was a hired gun, the Ryland lawmen brothers would find him, but Theo needed that to happen before the SOB managed to fire more shots at Kim and Faith. They'd been through enough.

Not just today but for the past twenty-one years.

Kim and Faith probably didn't care much for sharing a ditch with a dead man, especially a dead man who'd caused so much hell for them. Added to that, Faith was possibly in shock. Even after Theo had pulled her into a sitting position in the ditch, she'd kept her glassy eyes pinned to the man.

"I remembered it was Quill who took me," Faith muttered. "Too late, but I remembered."

"It wasn't too late," Kim assured her, and she pulled Faith into a hug. Something that Theo wanted to do to both of them, but he needed to keep watch. Carver was helping with that, but there were a lot of trees and shrubs that an attacker could use to sneak up on them.

"If I'd remembered sooner, Theo could have arrested him," Faith argued. But then she stopped and looked at both Kim and him. "And if that had happened, Quill would still be alive. I'm glad he's dead. I'm glad he'll never be able to come after us again."

Yeah, Theo wasn't shedding any tears over a killer getting a taste of his own medicine. And that caused him to think of Rowena, Nadia and Jack. Jack didn't even know Quill so he wouldn't be affected, and Nadia and her dad hadn't been close. Still, Nadia had lost her father, and she would have to deal with that. Theo would help her with it if she wanted.

Rowena would get his help, too. But Theo had to wonder if the woman would grieve for her dead husband, or would this be a relief for her, too? He thought that maybe, eventually, Rowena would be able to move on with her life and find her new normal.

He'd need to find a new normal as well. Heck, so would Kim and Faith. No way did he want to go back to the way things had been before. No. He needed both Kim and his sister in his life.

"Will you have to arrest me for killing Quill?" Faith asked.

Theo silently cursed and shook his head. "No. Quill had a gun and had taken Kim hostage. He would have killed all of us had he gotten the chance. You stopped him before he could do that."

Of course, Faith would have to live with the memory of doing that. Even though taking his life was justified, it would stay with her, and she'd never be the same. Of course, Quill had made sure she'd never be the same when he'd kidnapped her and handed her over to people who'd paid him to steal her from her family.

Faith blew out a long breath, maybe a little relieved that she wouldn't be arrested, and she leaned her head against the wall of the ditch. She was clearly exhausted, and once the adrenaline had run its course, she was going to crash. Maybe he'd have her safely out of there by then.

Kim, too.

Though she didn't look nearly as exhausted as his sister. In fact, she still seemed revved, but it might take a while for it to sink in just how close she'd come to dying tonight.

"I'm all right," Kim muttered, inching toward him. She didn't pull him into her arms, probably because she knew he was keeping watch, but she pressed her head against his shoulder. "Are you?"

"I'm getting there," he assured her, and having her this close to him was definitely helping.

She made a sound of agreement. "I know the timing for this sucks, but I need to tell you something. There was this thought that kept going through my head when Quill had me. I didn't want to die without letting you know how I feel about you. And how I feel about you is that I'm in love with you."

Her words hit him hard. Not in a punch-to-the-gut kind of way when he'd seen Quill dragging her away. No. This was a warmth that spread through him and immediately eased some of the dark places.

He didn't smile, or kiss her, though that's exactly what he wanted to do. Heck, he wanted to whoop for joy, but the dinging sound of his phone meant such things had to be put on hold.

We've got the shooter, Dade texted. *Just one. We found him at the back of the barn trying to get away. Grayson and Kade are dealing with him and will get him in a cell ASAP. By the way, he's a chatterbox and will confirm that Quill was the one who hired him.*

Now, the relief came, and rather than risk his voice, he showed Faith and Kim the message. Kim did whoop for joy, and she threw herself into his arms. Not a punch of warmth this time. It felt as if everything in his life moved into just the right place. Theo would have liked to have lingered there for, well, forever, but he had to send a reply to Dade to let him know their situation and location.

"It's over," Faith muttered. She was clearly relieved, too, and Kim reached out, pulling in both Theo and his sister to make it a group hug.

While he needed this—man, did he—Theo wanted to hear Kim repeat that part about being in love with him. Just so there was no doubt that she actually meant it. But he got another text before he could say anything.

It was Dade again.

We're on our way to you now. Mason's dealing with Greg and Rowena and will take them to the sheriff's office.

Good. That was one less thing for Theo to deal with. Mason could easily handle the pair and get them in for interviews. Both Rowena and Greg would need to be questioned to make sure they hadn't had a part in the murders and kidnappings. And even if Greg hadn't directly participated in those particular crimes, he was still guilty of not reporting that Ashley was Faith, something he'd admitted knowing if Quill was telling the truth about that.

Ava would be able to deal with that, along with giving Duran one final round in the interview room to be certain he hadn't done anything unlawful with his part in what was definitely an illegal adoption.

Since Quill had confessed and named the Neelys as the people who'd hired him, Rowena wouldn't be charged with those crimes. However, she could face charges for reckless endangerment for firing those shots at Greg.

Theo would also have to make it clear to Greg that even if he didn't end up in jail, he was to keep away from Faith. Well, keep away from her unless his sister changed her mind about that, but he was thinking that Greg was now a thing of the past for her.

Hopefully, a lot of things fell into that category for all of them.

Dade finally came out of the trees and started toward the ditch. He wasn't alone. Kim's father was with him, and Nate hurried to the ditch, no doubt to make sure his daughter was unharmed. Nate pulled up, though, right at the edge when he saw that Kim had her arm around Theo and she'd dropped her head on his shoulder. Nate lifted an eyebrow and shifted his attention to

Theo. Maybe Kim and he were sending off some kind of vibe, one not connected to what had just happened, because the corner of Nate's mouth lifted in a smile.

"About damn time," Nate muttered.

The knot in Theo's stomach loosened a bit. Not that he'd thought Kim's family wouldn't approve of them being together. He'd known they would. Still, it was good to have confirmation.

Dade helped Faith out of the ditch and then he dropped down next to Quill's body. "I can call for the medical examiner and the CSIs," he offered.

"And I can wait here with him," Nate added while he took hold of Kim's hand. He pulled her from the ditch and into his arms for a long hug. "Are you all right?" he murmured to his daughter.

"I'm better now," she settled for saying. "I don't think I have a scratch on me."

"Yeah, you do." Nate brushed his fingers over her chin. "I want to beat Quill to a pulp for doing that, but I think I'd have to stand in line. Theo would probably get first dibs."

Theo would take first dibs if Quill were still alive. He had a lot of anger for what the man had done to them and his family. But some of the anger melted away when Theo climbed out of the ditch and Kim moved away from her father to pull him into her arms. She didn't stop there. Nope.

She kissed him.

It wasn't tame. It was long, deep, and filled with relief, need. And love. Oh, yes. He felt all of that.

"I'm in love with Theo," Kim announced when she

finally took her mouth from his. "Anyone have a problem with that?"

There were some grumbled replies of approval. No objections, though, and Theo would have given those three words right back to her if his phone hadn't rung. Not one of the Rylands or deputies this time. It was Nadia.

Hell.

He certainly hadn't forgotten about his ex, but he hadn't wanted to talk to her until he'd had a chance to clear his head. Still, she'd maybe heard about the trouble at the ranch, and he didn't want her to be kept in the dark.

"Give me a minute," Theo said to no one in particular. He gave Kim a quick kiss and took the call.

"I heard there'd been a shooting at the old place," Nadia blurted out. "Are you all right?"

"I'm fine." Theo took hold of Kim's hand and moved her away from the others while Nate and Dade started checking Faith to make sure she hadn't been injured. "So is Faith." He paused, gathered his breath. "But Quill isn't. He's dead, Nadia. He's the one who killed my folks and kidnapped Faith."

He heard her gasp and was about to offer to go over there.

"He's responsible for the attacks?"

"Yes, and he tried to kidnap Kim just minutes ago." Theo would give her a more detailed account of events. If she wanted it, that is. "Rowena is all right, too, but she showed up as all of this was going down. She's being taken to the sheriff's office, if you want to see her."

"Is it safe for me to go out?" Nadia asked.

"It is. The Rylands captured the gunman Quill hired. But if you can hold off an hour or so, I can come over and take you to see your mother."

"Yes, please do that." She paused again. "Is Kim okay?"

"She is," Theo verified. "She's right here with me." Now it was his turn to pause. "I'd like to bring her with me to see Jack, if that's all right?"

Nadia took her time answering. "Yes, that'll be fine. I mean, Jack should get used to seeing you two together. You're in love with her?" Nadia tacked on.

Theo didn't want for Kim to hear those words from him while he was responding to his ex's question, so he went with a simple, "Yes."

He heard Nadia drag in a long breath. "All right. I'll see both of you when you come over."

Theo couldn't help it. He smiled. Nadia wasn't exactly jumping for joy over his feelings for Kim, but she wasn't hostile about them either. That was a good start. In fact, there'd been a lot of good starts today.

And that's why he ended the call, turned to Kim and kissed her.

He poured a lot of emotion into that kiss. A lot of hope, too. Because he had no doubts about his feelings for her, no doubts that he wanted her in his life.

The kiss lingered a lot longer than it should, especially considering this was a crime scene—with her father and uncles watching. Still, Theo had needed it. Judging from Kim's sound of pleasure, she had needed it as well.

He finally pulled back and looked her in the eyes.

Amazing eyes that he'd hopefully get to see every morning, every night.

Forever.

"I'm in love with you, Kim," Theo said. Not mere words but a promise.

She smiled, and though there were tears in her eyes, he knew these were happy ones. "Then, we're the luckiest people on earth because I'm in love with you. And you're going to need to say those words over and over to me again because I want to hear them a whole lot of times."

"No problem," Theo assured her. He could tell her he loved her, well, forever.

* * * * *

Look for the last book in USA TODAY
bestselling author Delores Fossen's
Silver Creek Lawmen: Second Generation when
Marked for Revenge *goes on sale next month!*

And if you missed the previous titles in the series,
you'll find Targeted in Silver Creek *and*
Maverick Detective Dad *wherever*
Harlequin Intrigue books are sold!

HARLEQUIN
PLUS

Try the best multimedia
subscription service for romance
readers like you!

Read, Watch and Play.

Experience the easiest way to get
the romance content you crave.

Start your **FREE TRIAL** at
<u>www.harlequinplus.com/freetrial</u>.